ALEX KNIGHT
AND THE
MULTIVERSE MAYHEM

Written By

ANDROR M. THOMPSON

ALEX KNIGHT
AND THE
MULTIVERSE MAYHEM

Contents

Esmeria Central Station
The Magical Forest
Esmeria Wonder Town
The Guardians of the Gardens

GUIDE TO WORLDS:
ESMERIA

CHAPTER ONE

SHADOWS OF THE PAST

Alex found himself standing in a dark, endless void, the kind where sound seemed to be swallowed by the oppressive silence. His breath echoed loudly, each exhale a desperate attempt to calm his pounding heart. He looked around, his eyes straining to see anything beyond the impenetrable darkness. He called out, but his voice was absorbed by the void, leaving him feeling even more isolated and vulnerable.

Suddenly, the darkness began to shift and swirl around him, forming a shape that he dreaded recognizing. A figure emerged, towering and ominous, with eyes that glowed a sinister red. It was Ruok, his arch-nemesis, the embodiment of all his fears. Ruok's presence radiated a malevolent energy that sent shivers down Alex's spine.

Alex tried to move, to run, but his legs felt like they were encased in cement. He was rooted to the spot, powerless and exposed. Ruok approached slowly, his lips curling into a sadistic grin.

"Did you think you could escape me, Alex?" Ruok's voice was a low, menacing growl. "You are nothing without your powers, just a mere mortal, and I will always find you."

Alex's heart raced. He tried to summon his abilities, the ones that had once made him a formidable opponent. But in this nightmare, he was stripped of his powers and reduced to a helpless bystander. He raised his hands defensively, but Ruok merely laughed, a cold, mocking sound that echoed through the void.

"Pathetic," Ruok sneered. "You think you can protect them? You can't even protect yourself."

With a swift, brutal motion, Ruok struck, and Alex felt the searing pain of defeat. He collapsed to the ground, his body trembling, his spirit crushed. Ruok leaned in close, his breath hot against Alex's ear.

"This is just the beginning," Ruok whispered. "I will destroy everything you hold dear."

Alex's scream echoed into the darkness as Ruok's laughter grew louder, more malevolent until it filled the entire void. Alex felt himself falling, endlessly falling, with no hope of escape.

Alex's scream continued to reverberate through the void, his mind grappling with the overwhelming fear and despair. He hit the ground hard, the impact jarring his senses. The void seemed to close in on him, the darkness becoming a tangible force pressing against his skin. He lay there, gasping for breath, trying to gather his thoughts and muster any semblance of strength.

Ruok's laughter echoed, reverberating through the void, a constant reminder of Alex's defeat. Alex struggled to push himself up, his limbs heavy and uncooperative. He felt a surge of anger mingled with his fear, a flicker of defiance amidst the overwhelming despair.

"Ruok," Alex spat, his voice trembling but determined. "You may think you've won, but this isn't over."

Ruok's laughter ceased abruptly, replaced by a chilling silence. He leaned down, his face inches from Alex's, those sinister red eyes boring into his soul.

"Oh, but it is over, Alex," Ruok whispered, his voice dripping with condescension. "You have nothing left. No powers, no allies, no hope. You're at my mercy."

Alex's eyes narrowed, a spark of defiance igniting within him. "I've faced worse than you, Ruok. And I've always found a way to fight back."

Ruok's grin widened, revealing sharp teeth that gleamed in the darkness. "Ah, the spirit of a warrior. How quaint. But spirit alone won't save you, Alex. You're in my world now, bound by my rules."

The void around them began to shift again, the darkness swirling with a malevolent energy. Images formed within the void, scenes from Alex's life, his failures and regrets, his moments of weakness and doubt. They played out like a cruel montage, each one a dagger to his heart.

"See how easily you break?" Ruok taunted. "Your mind is an open book to me, Alex. Every fear, every insecurity, laid bare. You can't hide from me."

Alex clenched his fists, his knuckles turning white. He forced himself to focus, to push through the mental onslaught. "You won't break me, Ruok. I've been broken before, and I've always come back stronger."

Ruok straightened, his expression shifting from amusement to mild irritation. "Stubbornness won't save you either. But let's test that resolve of yours, shall we?"

The void shifted again, this time revealing the faces of those Alex cared about—his friends, his family, those he had sworn to protect. They were trapped, bound in chains of shadow, their eyes filled with fear and desperation.

"Watch as I destroy everything you love," Ruok hissed. "One by one, I will break them, just as I have broken you."

Alex's heart pounded in his chest, his breath coming in ragged gasps. He struggled to rise, to do anything to stop the nightmare unfolding before him. But his body refused to cooperate, the weight of the void pressing down on him like an anchor.

"Leave them out of this," Alex pleaded, his voice raw with emotion. "This is between you and me."

Ruok chuckled darkly. "Oh, but you see, Alex, hurting them hurts you. And that's the point. To make you suffer. To make you realize the futility of your resistance."

Tears welled in Alex's eyes as he watched his loved ones suffer, their cries of pain piercing his heart. He felt a surge of helplessness, a crushing weight of failure. But amidst the despair, a flicker of determination remained. He couldn't let Ruok win. Not like this.

"You won't win," Alex said through gritted teeth. "I will find a way to stop you. I swear it."

Ruok's expression darkened, his eyes narrowing. "Bold words for a defeated man. Let's see how long that fire lasts."

The scene shifted again, the void morphing into a desolate wasteland. Alex found himself standing amidst ruins, the remnants of a world torn apart by chaos and destruction. Fires burned in the distance, the sky a dark, churning mass of storm clouds.

"This is your future, Alex," Ruok intoned. "A world where you failed. Where your defiance led to nothing but ruin."

Alex surveyed the devastation, his heart aching at the sight. But instead of despair, he felt a growing resolve. He knew this was a vision meant to break him, to strip away his hope. But hope was something he couldn't afford to lose.

"This isn't real," Alex said firmly. "This is just another one of your tricks."

Ruok appeared beside him, his presence a looming shadow. "Real or not, it's a reflection of what's to come if you continue to resist. Embrace the inevitable, Alex. Accept your place at my feet, and perhaps I'll show mercy to those you care about."

Alex turned to face Ruok, his eyes blazing with defiance. "I'll never bow to you. I'll fight you with every breath, every ounce of strength I have. You may think you can break me, but you're wrong."

Ruok's eyes flashed with anger, his calm façade slipping. "Then you will suffer, Alex. You and everyone you love."

With a wave of his hand, Ruok summoned a storm of shadows, the darkness swirling and converging around Alex. The shadows formed into twisted, nightmarish creatures, their eyes glowing with malevolence. They lunged at Alex, their claws raking at his skin, their snarls filling his ears.

Alex fought back with everything he had, his fists flying, his body moving on instinct. But the creatures were relentless, their numbers overwhelming. He felt himself being dragged down, the weight of the shadows suffocating.

But even as he fought, Alex's mind raced. He needed to find a way out, a way to turn the tide. He couldn't let Ruok win, not when so much was at stake.

Summoning every ounce of willpower, Alex forced himself to focus. He envisioned a light, a beacon of hope amidst the darkness. He concentrated on that light, willing it to grow, to pierce through the void.

The light flickered, then began to shine brighter, cutting through the shadows. The creatures recoiled, their forms dissipating in the face of the growing radiance.

"You can't break me, Ruok," Alex shouted, his voice echoing through the void. "I will find a way to defeat you. I will protect those I love."

Ruok snarled, his eyes blazing with fury. "This isn't over, Alex. I will return, and next time, you won't be so lucky."

With a final, ear-piercing scream, Ruok and the shadows vanished, leaving Alex alone in the void.

Alex jolted awake, his body drenched in sweat, his heart thundering in his chest. He sat up abruptly, gasping for air as if he had been drowning. The room was dark, but the familiar shapes of the furniture offered a small measure of comfort. He ran a trembling hand through his damp hair, trying to steady his breathing.

Beside him, Helen stirred her presence a soothing balm to his frayed nerves. She reached out, her touch gentle and reassuring. "Alex, it's okay," she whispered, her voice calm and soothing. "It's just a nightmare."

Alex turned to her, his eyes wide and haunted. "It felt so real, Helen. Ruok was there. He... he crushed me. I couldn't do anything."

Helen sat up, wrapping her arms around him. "Shh, it's all right. It was just a dream. Ruok hasn't come back. It's been a year since we last saw him."

"But what if he does come back?" Alex's voice was barely a whisper, his fear palpable. "What if he's just waiting for the right moment to strike?"

Helen gently cupped his face, forcing him to look into her eyes. "Listen to me, Alex. Ruok hasn't shown his face since that last encounter. You, Scarlette, and Marcus dealt with his inter-dimensional minions. If he was going to make a move, he would have done it by now. Maybe he was just bluffing."

Alex took a deep breath, trying to absorb her words. "Maybe you're right. Maybe it was just a bluff."

Helen nodded, her expression firm but loving. "You need to focus on the present, Alex. You're working hard at your job, and you're making progress with your writing. Don't let the past haunt you. We'll face whatever comes together like we always have."

Alex sighed, leaning into her embrace. "You're right, Helen. I just... I just can't shake the feeling sometimes."

Helen kissed his forehead, a tender gesture that spoke volumes. "I know. But we're stronger together. Remember that."

As Alex lay back down, his mind began to settle. Helen's steady presence beside him eased the lingering fear. He closed his eyes, willing himself to let go of the nightmare and focus on the reality of the life they had built together.

Alex stared at the ceiling, his thoughts a tumultuous sea of doubt and fear. He could feel the residual terror of the nightmare clinging to him, like a dark shroud he couldn't shake off. Helen's steady breathing beside him was a constant reminder of the calm he so desperately needed to embrace. He took a deep breath, drawing strength from her presence.

"Helen," he whispered, his voice barely audible. "What if it's more than just a nightmare? What if it's a warning?"

Helen turned to him, her eyes searching his. "Alex, we've talked about this. Your mind is still processing everything that happened. It's natural to have fears, especially after facing someone like Ruok. But you can't let those fears control you."

Alex sighed, his frustration mounting. "I know, but it feels like he's still out there, lurking, waiting for the right moment. What if we're not ready when he does strike?"

Helen's expression softened, her empathy shining through. "We'll never be completely ready for every challenge, Alex. But we've faced so much already. We've grown stronger together. And we're not alone. Scarlette and Marcus are with us. We have a support system."

Alex nodded, the tension in his shoulders easing slightly. "You're right. It's just... the thought of losing you, of losing everyone we care about. It's unbearable."

Helen squeezed his hand, her grip firm and reassuring. "We won't let that happen. We'll fight, just like we always have. And we'll do it together. That's what makes us strong, Alex. Our unity, our love for each other. Ruok can't take that away from us."

Alex's heart swelled with gratitude and love. Helen had always been his anchor, the one who kept him grounded even in the darkest times. He leaned in, pressing a gentle kiss to her lips. "Thank you, Helen. I don't know what I'd do without you."

Helen smiled, her eyes twinkling with affection. "You'd do just fine, but I'm glad you don't have to find out. Now, try to get some rest. We have a lot to do tomorrow, and you'll need your strength."

Alex nodded, feeling the exhaustion of the day and the nightmare finally catching up with him. He closed his eyes, allowing the rhythm of Helen's breathing to lull him into a more peaceful state. As sleep began to reclaim him, he made a silent vow to protect the life they had built together, no matter what challenges lay ahead.

The next morning, the sun streamed through the window, casting a warm glow over the room. Alex woke to the comforting scent of coffee brewing and the sound of birds chirping outside. He stretched.

Helen was already in the kitchen, humming softly as she prepared breakfast. Alex walked in, wrapping his arms around her from behind. "Good morning," he murmured, kissing her neck.

Helen smiled, leaning back into his embrace. "Good morning. Did you sleep better after our talk?"

Alex nodded, resting his chin on her shoulder. "I did. Thank you for being my rock, Helen. I don't know what I'd do without you."

Helen turned in his arms, her eyes filled with warmth. "You don't have to find out. We're in this together, remember?"

Alex kissed her, a slow, tender kiss that conveyed all the love and gratitude he felt. When they finally pulled apart, he felt lighter, more grounded. "Let's make today a good one," he said, determination shining in his eyes.

Helen nodded, her smile radiant. "Absolutely."

Alex made his way to Ryan's school, excitement and pride swelling in his chest. He had heard all about the new craze sweeping the schoolyards: Juggle Bubble. It was a fast-paced, thrilling game, and today, Ryan was playing in a highly anticipated match against a rival team led by the arrogant star player, Sebastian. Alex strolled toward the bleachers, his heart swelling with pride as he spotted his son, Ryan, warming up for the much-anticipated Juggle Bubble match.

Today, Ryan's team would face off against the school's top contender, led by the arrogant star player, Sebastian.

As the referee blew the whistle, signaling the start of the game, excitement buzzed through the crowd. The referee tossed two small, bouncy air balls, known as bubbles, into the air. Both teams' centers leapt up, and it was Ryan who caught the bubbles with an impressive display of agility. The game had begun.

Ryan quickly became a Juggler, deftly balancing the bubbles in his hands while weaving through the opposing team's Catchers. His teammates, acting as Catchers, flanked him, ready to receive a pass if necessary. The Catchers of Sebastian's team lunged at Ryan, but he skillfully dodged them, his eyes scanning for an opportunity to advance towards the goal.

"Watch out, Ryan!" shouted one of his teammates as a particularly aggressive Catcher closed in. Ryan swiftly tossed one bubble to his teammate, who immediately took on the role of Juggler. The fluid exchange was seamless, showcasing their well-practiced teamwork.

However, Sebastian, with his keen eyes and quick reflexes, managed to intercept a pass. He became the

Juggler, his movements a blur as he danced past Ryan and his team. The crowd roared as Sebastian approached the goal, but Ryan, determined not to let his team down, closed the distance between them.

Just as Ryan reached out to snatch the bubbles from Sebastian, a whistle blew sharply. The referee signaled a foul against Ryan for making contact. "That's one warning, Ryan!" the referee called out. The crowd groaned, and Alex winced from the sidelines.

Sebastian smirked, his confidence unshaken.

"Better luck next time, loser," he taunted, juggling the bubbles with infuriating ease.

Ryan gritted his teeth, focusing on the game. The referee threw the bubbles back into play, and the cycle continued.

The tension on the field was palpable, each team pushing their limits.

Ryan's determination only grew with each second, his movements becoming more precise.

The game progressed, with both teams showcasing impressive skills. Yet, fouls and warnings were inevitable.

One of Sebastian's teammates was disqualified for holding onto a Juggler, a clear violation. Despite this setback, Sebastian's team maintained their lead, largely due to his exceptional performance.

As the clock ticked down, Ryan's team managed to close the gap. With only a few minutes left, Ryan once again found himself as the Juggler, expertly maneuvering the bubbles. He saw an opening and made a dash towards the goal. Just as he was about to throw the bubbles, Sebastian appeared out of nowhere, swiping at the bubbles.

A whistle blew – foul on Sebastian! The crowd erupted, but the damage was done.

The referee retrieved the bubbles and threw them into the air again. This time, Sebastian's quick reflexes allowed him to gain possession. With a final, spectacular move, he hurled the bubbles into the goal, securing the victory for his team.

The game ended with the scoreboard flashing the final score. Ryan's shoulders slumped in disappointment as Sebastian strutted over, a smug grin plastered on his face.

"Told you, you'd never beat me," Sebastian sneered. "Better stick to watching from the sidelines."

Ryan's fists clenched, but before he could respond, his friend Jane, who had been watching the game intently, stepped in. Her eyes were bright with encouragement as she placed a comforting hand on Ryan's shoulder.

"Don't let him get to you, Ryan," she said softly. "You played amazingly well. Just ignore him."

Ryan looked at Jane, her words a balm to his wounded pride. He nodded, a small smile tugging at the corners of his mouth. "Thanks, Jane. I'll keep that in mind."

Ryan felt a surge of gratitude for Jane's encouragement, but his mind was still replaying the game, particularly Sebastian's smirk and taunting words. As they walked towards the changing rooms, Sebastian and a few of his teammates cut them off, blocking their path.

"Hey, Ryan," Sebastian called out, his voice dripping with mockery. "You put up a decent fight, I'll give you that. But honestly, did you really think you had a chance against me?"

Ryan clenched his fists, his knuckles whitening. "It was a fair game," he said evenly, trying to keep his anger in check. "We'll get you next time."

Sebastian laughed, a harsh, grating sound that echoed in the corridor. "Next time? Oh, that's rich. You might want to focus on getting through this season first. You'll never be able to handle the pressure."

Jane stepped forward, her eyes blazing. "Back off, Sebastian. Ryan played better than you today, and you know it. If it weren't for that foul, you wouldn't have won."

Sebastian's eyes narrowed as he turned his gaze to Jane. "Stay out of this, Jane. This is between me and the loser here." He jabbed a thumb towards Ryan. "Maybe you should spend less time cheering from the sidelines and more time practicing, Ryan. Or better yet, find a new hobby. One that doesn't involve embarrassing yourself in front of the whole school."

Ryan took a step forward, his anger boiling over. "You think you're so great, Sebastian? You're just a big fish in a small pond. One day, someone's going to come along and knock you off that pedestal you think you're so secure on."

Sebastian's grin widened, clearly enjoying the tension. "Oh, really? And you think you're the one to do it? You've got a long way to go, buddy. Maybe start by learning how to juggle properly without dropping the bubbles every other minute."

Ryan's face flushed with anger, but before he could respond, one of Sebastian's teammates, Mark, chimed in. "Yeah, Ryan. Maybe you should take some tips from Sebastian. Or better yet, just quit while you're ahead. Oh wait, you're not ahead. You're behind. Way behind."

Jane tightened her grip on Ryan's arm, trying to pull him back. "Let's go, Ryan. They're not worth it."

But Ryan shook his head, his eyes locked on Sebastian's. "You think you've won, Sebastian? This isn't over. We'll train harder, and we'll come back stronger. You can count on it."

Sebastian rolled his eyes, clearly unimpressed. "Whatever helps you sleep at night, Ryan. But remember, dreams don't win games. Skill does. And you're looking at the most skilled player this school has ever seen."

As Ryan's face lit up at the sight of his dad, Alex, approaching him, a small crowd began to gather around Alex, drawn by his aura of mystery and the whispered tales of his heroic exploits. Sebastian, however, couldn't hide his jealousy as the attention shifted away from him. He sneered at Alex, his tone dripping with sarcasm.

"Look who decided to grace us with his presence. Where are your powers now, Alex?" Sebastian taunted, his voice laced with disdain.

Alex's jaw clenched slightly at the disrespectful tone, but he remained composed, his gaze steady as he met Sebastian's challenging stare. "My powers are right where they need to be," he replied calmly, his voice carrying a hint of authority. He wasn't about to engage in a verbal sparring match with Sebastian, knowing that it would only escalate the situation.

Sebastian scoffed, his smirk widening. "Oh, come on, Alex. Don't tell me you've hung up your cape for good. I hope you're not as fake as Ryan here," he continued, his words a thinly veiled jab at both Alex and his son.

The crowd murmured in response, some casting curious glances at Alex, while others exchanged knowing looks. Jane, sensing Ryan's growing frustration, leaned in close and whispered in his ear, her voice a soothing reassurance. "Don't let him get to you, Ryan. He's just trying to rile you up," she advised, her words a gentle reminder to stay calm.

But Ryan's patience was wearing thin. His fists clenched at his sides as he took a step forward, his voice trembling with pent-up emotion. "You don't know anything about us, Sebastian. Don't you dare talk about my dad like that!" he snapped, his eyes blazing with indignation.

Alex placed a hand on Ryan's shoulder, his touch a silent plea for restraint. "Ryan, calm down," he said softly, his tone gentle but firm. He knew that escalating the situation further would only make things worse.

Sebastian, sensing Ryan's vulnerability, seized the opportunity to strike another blow. "What's the matter, Ryan? Can't handle a little criticism? Maybe you really are just a chip off the old block," he taunted, his smirk widening into a smug grin.

Ryan's temper flared at the insult, his fists tightening even further. Before Alex could intervene, Ryan lunged at Sebastian, his anger boiling over into action. The crowd erupted into chaos as Alex tried to pull Ryan away from the confrontation, but it was too late. The commotion drew the attention of nearby families and opposing supporters, who gathered around, their phones held aloft to capture the spectacle.

Amidst the chaos, Alex felt a surge of frustration. He never liked being the center of attention, especially when it involved his past as a hero. With a sigh, he managed to break free from the crowd, guiding Ryan outside and towards their car. The sounds of shouting and jeering faded into the distance as they made their escape, leaving behind the chaos of the confrontation.

As they reached the car, Alex's frustration boiled over, and he turned to Ryan with a stern expression. "Ryan, what were you thinking? That was completely unacceptable!" he snapped, his voice tinged with disappointment.

Ryan bristled at his father's tone, his own anger still simmering beneath the surface. "Me? What about Sebastian? He's the one who started it!" he shot back, his voice tinged with defiance.

Alex sighed heavily, running a hand through his hair in frustration. "I don't care who started it, Ryan. You know better than to resort to violence. We've talked about this before," he said, his voice tinged with exasperation.

Ryan's shoulders slumped, the weight of his father's disappointment settling heavily upon him. "I know, Dad. I'm sorry," he muttered, his voice barely above a whisper.

Alex's expression softened slightly as he saw the remorse in Ryan's eyes. He reached out, placing a comforting hand on his son's shoulder. "I know you are, Ryan. But you need to understand that violence is never the answer. It only leads to more problems," he said, his voice gentle but firm.

Ryan nodded slowly, his gaze fixed on the ground as he absorbed his father's words. "I know, Dad. I just...I couldn't let him talk about you like that," he admitted, his voice thick with emotion.

Alex's heart clenched at the raw honesty in Ryan's words. He knew that his son looked up to him, admired him even, and the thought of anyone tarnishing that image filled him with a fierce protectiveness. "Ryan, you don't have to defend me. I can handle myself," he said, his voice tinged with sadness.

Ryan looked up, his eyes searching his father's face for reassurance. "But why didn't you say anything, Dad? Why didn't you tell them about your adventures?" he asked, his voice tinged with confusion.

Alex's heart ached at the question, the memories of his past weighing heavily upon him. "Because that part of my life is over, Ryan. It's in the past," he replied, his voice tinged with regret.

Ryan's brow furrowed in confusion. "But why, Dad? Why can't you be a hero again?" he asked, his voice tinged with longing.

Alex sighed heavily, struggling to find the right words to explain. "Because being a hero comes with a cost, Ryan. And sometimes, that cost is too high," he said, his voice tinged with sorrow.

Ryan sighed disheartened, the reality of his father's words sinking in.

"I understand, Dad. I just wish things were different," he admitted, his voice tinged with sadness.

Alex reached out, pulling Ryan into a tight embrace. "I know, son. But sometimes, we have to accept things as they are and focus on what's important – our family and friends," he said, his voice tinged with warmth.

Ryan nodded slowly, feeling a sense of comfort wash over him in his father's embrace. "I know, Dad. I'm sorry for snapping at you," he muttered, his voice tinged with regret.

Alex smiled gently, brushing a stray lock of hair from Ryan's forehead. "It's okay, Ryan. I understand. Just remember what I said – violence is never the answer. It's best to just ignore and walk away," he said, his voice tinged with wisdom.

Ryan nodded solemnly, a sense of determination settling over him. "I will, Dad. I promise," he said, his voice tinged with resolve.

The tension between them slowly dissipated as they drove away from the school.

Later that night, Scarlette, a determined and skilled police officer, was on patrol. The city was quiet, but her instincts told her something was off. Her partner was in the passenger seat, scanning the streets for any signs of trouble.

"Do you ever get the feeling that something big is about to happen?" Scarlette asked, her eyes focused on the road ahead.

Her partner raised an eyebrow, smirking. "With you around, Scarlette, I always expect something big to happen."

Scarlette rolled her eyes playfully. "Very funny. But seriously, I just have this gut feeling."

Before her partner could respond, a call came through the radio. "All units, be advised. We have a suspect fleeing on foot near 5th and Maple. Requesting immediate backup."

Scarlette's eyes lit up with determination. "That's us. Let's go." She flipped on the siren and sped towards the location, adrenaline pumping through her veins.

When they arrived, they saw a man darting down an alley, his silhouette barely visible in the dim streetlights. Scarlette sprang into action, chasing after the suspect with her partner close behind.

The suspect was fast, leaping over fences and walls with an agility that surprised even Scarlette. She pushed herself harder, her breaths coming in sharp bursts as she tried to keep up.

"He's heading towards the warehouse district!" her partner shouted, struggling to keep pace.

Scarlette's mind raced. She couldn't let this guy get away. Suddenly, she felt a strange sensation in her back, a heat that spread through her shoulders. The feeling was intense, almost burning, but she pushed it aside, focusing on the chase.

"Don't lose him!" her partner yelled, his voice echoing in the narrow alleyways.

"I'm not planning on it!" Scarlette shot back, her determination only growing stronger. The suspect was gaining distance, his movements a blur in the dim light. Scarlette's heart pounded in her chest as she pushed her legs to move faster, but it felt like the suspect was slipping away.

As they neared the warehouse district, the buildings and alleyways made keeping track of the suspect even harder. Scarlette's frustration mounted, her breaths coming in ragged gasps. She couldn't let him escape, not now.

Suddenly, the burning sensation in her back intensified, becoming almost unbearable. Scarlette stumbled, momentarily losing her footing. Her partner glanced back, concern etched on his face.

"Scarlette, are you okay?" he called out, slowing down slightly.

"Yeah, just... keep going!" she gasped, trying to push through the pain. But then something incredible happened. With a sudden burst of energy, two large, crimson wings erupted from her back, unfurling with a dazzling display of red feathers. Scarlette felt a surge of power course through her veins as she rose into the air, propelled by the wings that had somehow manifested from within her.

Her partner's eyes widened in shock. "What the...?"

Scarlette didn't have time to explain. She soared above the alley, spotting the suspect below as he darted between the buildings. She swooped down with a powerful beat of her wings, cutting off his escape route. The suspect skidded to a halt, eyes wide with terror as he stared up at the sight before him.

"You're not going anywhere," Scarlette declared, her voice firm and unwavering. She landed gracefully in front of the suspect, her wings folding behind her as she advanced on him. The man tried to back away, but Scarlette was too quick. With a swift, practiced motion, she had him on the ground, handcuffs clicking into place around his wrists.

A small crowd had gathered, drawn by the commotion. They watched in stunned silence, their faces reflecting a mix of awe and disbelief. Scarlette could hear whispers spreading through the crowd, but she blocked them out, focusing on the task at hand.

"You have the right to remain silent," she began, reciting the familiar words with a new sense of authority. "Anything you say can and will be used against you in a court of law..."

Her partner finally caught up, panting heavily. He stared at Scarlette, his expression a mix of astonishment and confusion. "Scarlette, what just happened? How did you...?"

"I don't know," Scarlette admitted, her voice trembling slightly. "I don't know how or why, but... I think I can manipulate and manifest red things."

Her partner shook his head, still trying to process what he had seen. "That's... incredible. And kind of terrifying."

Scarlette nodded, feeling a mix of emotions swirling inside her. She was shocked, embarrassed by the attention, but also strangely exhilarated. She had discovered a power within herself that she never knew existed, and it had just saved the day.

As they led the suspect to the police car, Scarlette could feel the eyes of her colleagues and the crowd on her, their silence speaks volumes. She tried to ignore the stares, focusing instead on the suspect and the job at hand. But deep down, she knew that everything had changed. She had a new power, and with it, a new responsibility.

Her partner finally broke the silence as they drove back to the station. "So, what now? Are you going to tell the chief about... this?"

Scarlette sighed, staring road ahead of her, filled with uncertainty and challenges.

Her partner turned to her with a thoughtful expression. "Scarlette, have you ever wondered why this happened to you? I mean, there must be a reason, right?"

Scarlette paused, considering his words. "I've thought about it a lot. I don't have any answers, but maybe it's not about why it happened. Maybe it's about what I choose to do with it."

Her partner nodded, a smile playing on his lips. "That's a good way to look at it. And from what I've seen, you're going to do some amazing things."

Scarlette smiled, feeling a sense of warmth and gratitude. "Thanks. I just want to make sure I use this power for good. To help people."

"You will," her partner assured her. "I do not doubt that."

Their conversation was interrupted by a sudden call over the radio.

Alex paced back and forth in the living room, his frustration evident in the rigid tension of his shoulders. Helen sat on the edge of the couch, her arms crossed, eyes following Alex's every movement.

"I just don't understand why you can't see it from his perspective," Helen began, her voice carrying a mixture of exasperation and concern.

"Ryan needs to show people that his Dad is indeed the legendary Alex Knight. It's not just about proving something to his peers; it's about his identity."

Alex stopped pacing and turned to face her, his expression softening slightly.

"Helen, I get it. I do. But he shouldn't have to rely on my past to define his present. Ryan needs to find his strength, his path. He shouldn't have to use my history to shield himself from bullies or to validate his worth."

Helen's brow furrowed. "It's not just about validation. It's about protection. If they see that he's your son, they might back off. Sebastian and his cronies won't be so quick to taunt him if they know he comes from a family of—"

"A family of what, Helen?" Alex interrupted, his tone sharper than he intended. "A family of heroes? That's not fair to Ryan.

He shouldn't have to live in my shadow. He needs to learn that he has greatness within him, just like I did when I was a kid. But it has to be his own greatness, not a reflection of mine."

Helen sighed, uncrossing her arms and leaning forward. "I understand that, Alex. I do. But have you considered how hard it is for him? He's trying to find his place in a world where everyone knows who his father is. That's a lot of pressure for a kid."

Alex ran a hand through his hair, his frustration giving way to a pained look. "I know it's hard. I know he's struggling. But using my legacy as a crutch isn't going to help him in the long run. He needs to build his own confidence, his own reputation. If he doesn't, he'll always feel inadequate, always feel like he's living in my shadow."

Helen nodded slowly, her gaze softening. "You're right, Alex. He does need to find his own way. But he also needs our support, and sometimes that means using the tools at his disposal. If showing that he's your son can help him now, maybe we should let him use that until he finds his footing."

Alex sat down beside her, taking her hand in his. "We can support him without letting him rely too heavily on my past. We need to find a balance. Encourage him to be proud of who he is, not just who his father is."

Helen squeezed his hand gently. "I admit, you have a point. Ryan does need to learn to stand on his own. But we need to make sure he knows that we're here for him, no matter what. That he has our support as he finds his own path."

Alex nodded, a small smile tugging at the corners of his mouth. "We'll figure it out together. We'll help him see that he has the same potential for greatness that we see in him."

Helen smiled back, her eyes glistening with unshed tears. "Yes, we will. For now, let's just make sure he knows he's loved and supported. That's the most important thing."

The air in the living room felt charged, the weight of their words hanging between them. Alex took a deep breath, feeling the need to clarify his thoughts more precisely.

"Helen, you know what it was like for me growing up," Alex said, his voice softer now, filled with memories. "I didn't have a legendary father to fall back on. I had to prove myself, to find my own way. And yes, it was tough, but it made me who I am."

Helen looked at him, her eyes filled with understanding and something deeper—a shared history. "And that's exactly why you can guide Ryan now. He can learn from your experiences. But Alex, he's not you. His challenges are different, and the world has changed."

Alex nodded thoughtfully. "You're right. Times have changed, and maybe I'm being too hard on him. But I don't want him to feel like he's less of a person if he's not living up to some image of me."

Helen reached out and placed a hand on Alex's arm, her touch warm and grounding.

"He won't, Alex. Not if we remind him every day that he's valued for who he is. That he doesn't have to be you to be great."

Alex sighed, his shoulders relaxing a bit. "I just wish he could see that he's strong in his own right. I don't want him to feel like he has to prove anything to anyone, especially not to Sebastian."

"Sebastian is a bully," Helen said firmly. "And Ryan needs to know that bullies are often insecure themselves. If Ryan can learn to stand up to him without relying on your name, it'll be a victory for him."

Alex leaned back, staring at the ceiling for a moment before looking back at Helen. "Maybe we need to talk to Ryan more. Help him see his own strengths. Encourage him to pursue his own interests and passions, not just what he thinks will impress others."

Helen smiled. "That sounds like a plan. And we should also make sure he knows that it's okay to ask for help. That asking for help doesn't mean he's weak."

Alex returned her smile, feeling a bit of the tension ease out of him. "Agreed. We should let him know that he can come to us with anything, no matter how small it seems."

Helen stood up, pulling Alex with her. "Let's go talk to him now. It's better to address this sooner rather than later."

They walked up the stairs together, the house quiet except for the soft hum of the refrigerator and the occasional creak of the floorboards. As they approached Ryan's room, they could hear the faint sound of video game music filtering through the closed door.

Alex knocked gently before pushing the door open. Ryan looked up from his game, his eyes widening slightly in surprise. "Hey, Mom. Dad."

"Hey, bud," Alex said, sitting down on the edge of Ryan's bed. Helen joined him, her hand resting lightly on Ryan's shoulder.

"We wanted to talk to you," Helen began, her voice gentle but serious. "About everything that's been going on at school. About Sebastian and the other kids."

Ryan's expression shifted, a mixture of defensiveness and resignation. "I know what you're going to say. I should just ignore them, right?"

Alex shook his head. "Not exactly. Ignoring them isn't always the best option. We want you to understand that you don't have to prove anything to them. You don't have to show them who your dad is to get them to back off."

Ryan's eyes flicked to Alex, searching his father's face for something. "But they keep saying I'm weak, that I'm nothing."

Helen squeezed his shoulder. "You're not nothing, Ryan. You're everything to us. And you have your own strengths, your own abilities. You don't need to use your dad's name to show them that."

"But it's so hard," Ryan admitted, his voice cracking slightly. "Sometimes it feels like I'll never be good enough."

Alex's heart ached hearing his son's vulnerability. He leaned forward, his voice filled with sincerity. "Ryan, listen to me. You are more than good enough. You have the same potential for greatness that anyone else has. You have your own path to follow, and we're here to help you every step of the way."

Ryan looked down at his hands, fiddling with the edge of his shirt. "I just... I just don't want them to think I'm a loser."

Helen brushed a lock of hair from Ryan's forehead, her touch gentle and loving. "You're not a loser, sweetheart. You're our son, and we're so proud of you. And you know what? Those kids who are mean to you? They're the ones who are struggling with their own insecurities. You don't need to prove anything to them."

Alex nodded in agreement. "We want you to be confident in who you are, not who you think you should be because of me. You have your own strengths, your own talents. Let's find those together."

Ryan looked up, a spark of hope in his eyes. "Okay. I guess I can try."

Helen smiled warmly. "That's all we ask. And remember, you can always come to us. We're here for you, no matter what."

Alex wrapped an arm around his son, pulling him into a comforting hug. "We're in this together, buddy. Always."as they walked out of his room.

Ryan lay on his bed, staring up at the ceiling. The conversation with his parents had helped, but he still felt a gnawing frustration. He picked up his phone and dialed Jane's number. She answered on the second ring.

"Hey, Ryan," Jane's cheerful voice came through the speaker. "What's up?"

Ryan sighed heavily. "Hey, Jane. Just needed to vent. You have a minute?"

"Of course," Jane replied. "What's going on?"

"It's this stupid Jugglebubble game," Ryan began, running a hand through his hair. "I just can't seem to get the hang of it, and Sebastian and his gang keep rubbing it in my face. And on top of that, my dad... I just don't get why he isn't more proud of his heroic history. I mean, he was a legend, right? Why doesn't he want to talk about it?"

Jane paused, thinking carefully before she spoke. "Ryan, your dad has his reasons. You need to be more understanding about it. Everyone has parts of their past they might not want to constantly relive, even if they were heroic."

Ryan frowned, frustration bubbling up again. "But it feels like he's ashamed of it or something. Like he's not proud of what he did."

"I don't think it's that," Jane said gently. "I think it's more about wanting you to forge your own path. He doesn't want you to feel like you have to live up to his past. And honestly, a loss in a Jugglebubble game doesn't define who you are as a person."

Ryan let out a breath he didn't realize he was holding. "I know, but it's hard not to feel like a loser when they keep reminding me of it."

"Ryan, you're not a loser," Jane said firmly. "You're smart, you're kind, and you have so much potential. Sebastian is just trying to get under your skin. Don't let him."

Ryan felt a small smile tug at his lips. "Thanks, Jane. Talking to you always helps."

"That's what friends are for," Jane replied. "And remember, you don't have to prove anything to anyone. Be proud of who you are, not just because of your dad's history."

Ryan nodded, even though she couldn't see him. "Yeah, you're right. It's just... I still want to show Sebastian that I'm not weak. That I'm not a loser."

Jane's voice was thoughtful. "There are better ways to show strength than winning at a game, Ryan. Show them through your actions, your character. Stand up for yourself and others, be confident in who you are. That's true strength."

Ryan's smile grew. "You always know what to say. Thanks, Jane."

"Anytime," Jane said warmly. "And hey, maybe we can practice Jugglebubble together sometime. Two heads are better than one, right?"

Ryan chuckled. "Yeah, that sounds good. Thanks again, Jane."

"Anytime, Ryan. See you at school tomorrow?"

"Yeah, see you tomorrow."

Ryan hung up the phone feeling lighter. Jane always had a way of putting things into perspective. He knew he still had a lot to figure out, but for now, he felt a bit more at ease. He wasn't alone in this. He had his parents, and he had Jane. And maybe, just maybe, that was enough.

As he lay there, he thought more about what Jane had said. It was true that his dad's past was a big part of their family history, but it didn't have to overshadow everything he did.

Ryan thought about his own interests and talents. He loved drawing, and he was pretty good at it too. Maybe he could focus more on that, show his worth through his art.

Just then, his phone buzzed with a new message. It was from Jane.

Hey, I know you're feeling down, but remember the school art competition coming up? Why don't you enter? I bet you'd do great!

Ryan read the message and felt a surge of excitement. He had completely forgotten about the competition. He quickly typed back.

Thanks, Jane. That's a great idea! I'll start working on something tonight.

Awesome! Can't wait to see what you come up with. You're going to rock it!

Ryan put his phone down, feeling a renewed sense of purpose. He got up from his bed and headed to his desk, pulling out his sketchbook and pencils. He began to sketch, letting his creativity flow. For the first time in days, he felt truly at peace. He didn't need to prove anything to Sebastian or anyone else. He just needed to be himself.

Later that night, as Helen was brushing her teeth, Alex found himself in the study. The room was filled with mementoes of his past adventures in Esmeria. On one of the shelves, old photographs and books chronicling his days as part of the Realm Defenders caught his eye. He reached up and pulled down a dusty photo album, flipping through its pages.

Images of his younger self with Marcus and Scarlette stared back at him. The trio looked fearless and invincible, ready to take on any challenge that Esmeria threw their way.

They had been through so much together – battling dark wizards and saving entire kingdoms.

Each picture told a story, each page a memory.

Alex sighed, a mix of nostalgia and pride swelling within him. He smiled to himself as he remembered the adventures that had defined a significant part of his life.

Helen emerged from the bathroom, her hair wrapped in a towel. She noticed Alex standing by the bookshelf, the photo album open in his hands. She walked over and peered over his shoulder, her eyes softening as she saw the images.

"Those were some incredible times," Helen said, her voice warm with reminiscence. "You all look so young and full of life."

Alex nodded, closing the album but not putting it down. "We were," he said quietly. "Those were some of the best years of my life. But they were also some of the hardest. It's funny how time makes you remember the good moments more vividly than the bad ones."

Helen slipped her arm around his waist. "It's natural to feel nostalgic, Alex. Those experiences shaped who you are today."

He turned to look at her, a tender smile on his face. "I know. And I'm grateful for everything we went through. But sometimes I wonder if I'm doing the right thing by not sharing more of it with Ryan."

Helen reached up and touched his cheek gently. "You're doing what you think is best for him. And that's all any parent can do."

They stood there in silence for a moment, surrounded by the artefacts of Alex's past.

Helen glanced at the books on the shelf, titles like "Alex Knight & The Realm Defenders" catching her eye. She smiled and squeezed his hand.

"You know," she said, "we should catch up with Marcus and Scarlette again. It's been too long since we've seen them."

Alex's eyes lit up at the suggestion. "That's a great idea. I miss them. It would be good to reconnect."

Helen nodded. "And who knows? Maybe hearing more about your past from them could help Ryan understand it better. Sometimes it helps to get different perspectives."

Alex pondered this for a moment. "You're right. I think it would do all of us some good. I'll give them a call tomorrow."

Helen smiled and leaned in to kiss him. "I think that sounds like a wonderful plan."

Ryan continued to work on his drawing late into the night. The sketch was coming together beautifully – a dragon soaring over a medieval castle, its wings spread wide against a stormy sky.

As he added the final touches, he felt a sense of accomplishment wash over him. He couldn't wait to show Jane and his parents.

CHAPTER TWO

THE CREATIVE RYAN

The next morning, Ryan woke up early, excitement bubbling within him. He carefully packed his sketchbook into his backpack, making sure the drawing was secure. He rushed downstairs to find his parents in the kitchen, sipping their coffee.

"Morning, Mom! Morning, Dad!" Ryan greeted them cheerfully.

Alex looked up from his mug, surprised at his son's upbeat mood. "Good morning, Ryan. You're up early."

Ryan grinned. "Yeah, I was working on a drawing last night for the school art competition. I wanted to show you guys before I head to school."

Helen's eyes sparkled with interest. "Oh, that's wonderful, Ryan! Let's see it."

Ryan pulled out his sketchbook and carefully opened it to the page with his drawing. He laid it on the kitchen table, watching his parents' reactions closely.

Alex and Helen leaned in, examining the intricate details of the dragon and the castle. Alex's eyes widened in admiration. "Ryan, this is incredible. You have a real talent for this."

Helen nodded in agreement. "It's beautiful, sweetheart. I'm so proud of you."

Ryan beamed with pride. "Thanks, Mum. Thanks, Dad. Jane reminded me about the competition, and I thought it would be a good way to show what I can do."

Alex smiled, a thought occurring to him. "You know, Ryan, your drawing reminds me of some of the creatures we faced back in Esmeria. Have I ever told you about the time Marcus, Scarlette, and I fought a dangerous carnivorous plant in the "Ludicrous Legumes" world with a holographic sword?"

Ryan's eyes widened with curiosity. "No, you haven't! I'd love to hear about it."

Helen and Alex exchanged a glance. "Well," Alex began, "it was one of our toughest battles. The dangerous carnivorous plant in the "Ludicrous Legumes" was guarding a treasure, and we had to work together to outsmart it with a holographic sword. Marcus was the strategist, Scarlette handled the magic, and I..."

As Alex recounted the tale, Ryan listened with rapt attention. He could almost picture his dad, Marcus, and Scarlette facing the formidable beast.

For the first time, he felt a connection to his father's past that wasn't overshadowed by expectations or comparisons.

Later that afternoon, Ryan met up with Jane at their usual spot by the school courtyard. He pulled out his sketchbook, eager to show her the finished drawing.

"Wow, Ryan!" Jane exclaimed, her eyes wide with admiration. "This is amazing! You're going to win the competition."

Ryan blushed, pleased with her reaction. "Thanks, Jane. I couldn't have done it without your encouragement."

Jane smiled warmly. "That's what friends are for. And hey, I'm here to help you practice Jugglebubble too.

Let's show Sebastian what we're made of."

Ryan grinned. "Sounds like a plan. Let's do it."

As the school day ended, Ryan felt a sense of contentment he hadn't felt in a long time. He had his friends, his family, and his unique talents. And for the first time, he didn't feel the need to prove anything to anyone. He was enough, just as he was.

That evening, after dinner, Alex made a phone call to Marcus. The conversation was filled with laughter and reminiscing about old times. They made plans to meet up the following weekend, and Alex felt a sense of excitement about reconnecting with his old friends.

The weekend couldn't come soon enough. When Saturday finally arrived, Ryan and his parents drove to a cosy café in the city where they had arranged to meet Marcus and Scarlette. As they walked in, Alex spotted them sitting at a corner table, waving enthusiastically.

Marcus stood up first, his tall frame and broad shoulders as imposing as ever. His face broke into a wide grin as he saw Alex. "Alex! It's been too long!"

Alex embraced his old friend warmly. "Marcus, you haven't changed a bit."

Scarlette, with her striking hair and sharp eyes, joined the hug. "Alex, it's so good to see you!"

They exchanged greetings, and introductions were made. Ryan found himself staring in awe at the people who had been such a big part of his father's legendary past.

"It's great to finally meet you, Ryan," Marcus said, shaking his hand firmly. "Your dad's told us so much about you."

Ryan smiled shyly. "Nice to meet you too."

As they sat down, the conversation flowed naturally. They talked about their current lives, reminisced about old adventures, and shared plenty of laughs. Ryan found himself fascinated by the stories

Marcus and Scarlette told, each one filled with excitement and danger.

"You know," Scarlette said, turning to Ryan, "your dad was one of the bravest people I've ever known. He always put others before himself."

Ryan looked at his dad, a new sense of pride swelling within him. "Really?"

Alex smiled, a bit embarrassed by the praise. "We were a team. We couldn't have done it without each other."

The afternoon passed quickly, filled with stories and memories. Ryan felt like he was seeing a whole new side of his father, one that he could respect and admire without feeling overshadowed.

As they prepared to leave, Marcus put a hand on Ryan's shoulder. "Remember, Ryan, it's not about living up to anyone else's expectations. It's about finding your path and being true to yourself."

Scarlette nodded. "And if you ever need advice or just want to hear more stories, you know where to find us."

Ryan nodded, feeling grateful for their kindness.

"Thanks, I appreciate it."

On the drive home, Ryan couldn't stop thinking about everything he had heard. He realized that his father's past was a part of who he was, but it didn't define him. He had his strengths, his talents, and his journey to follow.

"Hey, Ryan," Alex said, sitting down next to him. "How's the drawing coming along?"

Ryan looked up and smiled. "It's going well, Dad. Thanks for asking."

Alex nodded, glancing at the drawing. "It looks fantastic. You have a talent for this."

Ryan felt a warm glow of pride. "Thanks, Dad. I've been thinking a lot about what you and Jane said. About finding my path."

Alex smiled a hint of pride in his eyes. "I'm glad to hear that. You're doing great, Ryan. Just keep being true to yourself."

The day of the school art competition arrived, and Ryan felt a mix of excitement and nervousness. He had worked hard on his pieces, and he was proud of what he had created. As he set up his display, he noticed other students doing the same, each one showcasing their unique talents.

Jane walked over to him, her face beaming with excitement. "Ryan, your display looks amazing!"

Ryan smiled, feeling a surge of confidence. "Thanks, Jane. I'm really happy with how it turned out."

As the judges made their rounds, Ryan's parents arrived, joining him and Jane. They admired the artwork, each piece telling a different story.

When the results were announced, Ryan held his breath. He didn't win first place, but he did receive an honourable mention for his dragon drawing. The recognition felt good, but what mattered more was the journey he had taken to get there.

After the competition, as they walked back to the car, Alex put an arm around Ryan's shoulders. "I'm so proud of you, Ryan. Not just for your art, but for how you've grown."

Ryan looked up at his dad, a smile spreading across his face. "Thanks, Dad. I couldn't have done it without you and Mom. And Jane, of course."

Helen squeezed his hand. "We're always here for you, sweetheart. No matter what."

As they drove home, Ryan looked out the window, thinking about his future. He knew that he would face more obstacles and moments of doubt, but he also knew that he had the strength and support to overcome them.

And with that thought, he felt ready to face whatever came next. He was enough, just as he was.

And that was more than enough, after the excitement of the day had settled, Ryan found himself back in his room, reflecting on everything that had happened. He picked up his sketchbook and began to draw, letting his thoughts and feelings flow onto the paper. It was a scene of a young boy standing at the edge of a cliff, looking out over a vast, beautiful landscape. The boy's expression was one of determination and hope, ready to embark on his adventure.

As he worked on the drawing, he heard a knock on his door. "Come in," he called out.

Alex stepped into the room, carrying a small box.

"Hey, Ryan. I have something for you."

Ryan looked up, curious. "What is it, Dad?"

Alex handed him the box. "I thought you might like this. It's something from my past, but I think it could inspire you."

Ryan opened the box and found a beautifully crafted compass inside. The metal was worn with age, but it still had a certain elegance to it. "This is amazing," he said, turning the compass over in his hands.

Alex smiled.

Ryan felt a lump in his throat. "Thank you, Dad. This means a lot."

Alex hugged him tightly. "You're welcome, son. I believe in you, and I know you'll do great things."

As Alex left the room, Ryan placed the compass on his desk.

In St James Park, London, the serene afternoon was interrupted by a disturbance that seemed almost otherworldly. The sky above the park was a perfect, clear blue, contrasting sharply with the unnatural shimmer that appeared near the lake. A young couple, enjoying a picnic, were the first to notice it. The boyfriend intrigued, squinted and pointed towards the strange phenomenon.

"Do you see that?" he asked, curiosity evident in his voice.

The girlfriend followed his gaze and gasped. "What is it?" she asked, her voice tinged with unease.

"I don't know," he replied, standing up. "But I'm going to find out."

As he approached the shimmering air, the distortion grew more pronounced, taking on the form of a swirling vortex. Without warning, a creature stepped through—a kelpie, a mythical horse-like beast, its dark mane dripping with water, eyes glowing with an eerie light. The creature's sudden appearance seemed to distort reality around it, making the air hum with an unnatural energy.

The boyfriend pulled out his phone, eager to capture this unbelievable sight. "This is incredible," he murmured, more to himself than to his girlfriend, who remained rooted to the picnic blanket, fear paralyzing her.

"Be careful!" she called out, her voice trembling.

But he was too engrossed in his discovery. Slowly, he crept closer, his phone held up to record every detail of the kelpie. The creature's eyes fixed on him, and for a moment, it seemed almost peaceful, as if it was merely curious about the strange world it had entered.

"Look at this," he whispered, glancing back at his girlfriend with a grin. "It's like something out of a fantasy novel."

He took another step forward, his phone capturing the kelpie's every move. The creature's ears twitched, and it lowered its head, sniffing the air. The moment felt frozen in time, a delicate balance between two worlds. Then, in an instant, the kelpie's demeanour changed. Its eyes flared with a sudden, terrifying hunger, and it lunged.

"Run!" the girlfriend screamed, but it was too late.

The kelpie's jaws snapped shut around the boyfriend, pulling him into its maw with a horrifying swiftness. His scream was cut short, and the phone fell to the ground, still recording the gruesome scene. The girlfriend watched in horror as the creature devoured him, the reality of the situation crashing down on her with brutal force.

She scrambled to her feet, her picnic forgotten, and ran, her screams echoing through the park. Her heart pounded in her chest, each beat a frantic drum urging her to move faster, to escape the nightmare that had shattered their peaceful afternoon.

As she ran, she glanced back and saw the kelpie standing over the remains of the picnic, its eyes following her with a cold, calculating gaze. She pushed herself harder, darting through the trees, her mind racing. She had to find help, had to warn others about the creature that had invaded their world.

Her flight brought her to a nearby path where a few park-goers were strolling, oblivious to the terror that had unfolded. She stumbled towards them, gasping for breath, her words tumbling out in a frantic rush.

"Help! Please, there's a monster! It killed my boyfriend!"

The people turned to her, their expressions shifting from confusion to concern. One of them, an older man, stepped forward. "Calm down, miss. What happened?"

"A creature," she sobbed, pointing back the way she came. "A horse-like monster. It came through a portal and attacked us."

The man's brow furrowed in scepticism, but the sheer panic in her eyes made him pause. "Where did this happen?" he asked, trying to make sense of her story.

"By the lake," she managed to say, her voice breaking. "It's still there. We have to call the police!"

The group hesitated, exchanging uncertain glances. But the desperation in her plea was undeniable. One of them pulled out a phone and dialed emergency services, while the others tried to comfort her.

As they waited, the girlfriend kept looking over her shoulder, expecting to see the kelpie at any moment. She shivered, her mind replaying the horrific scene over and over. The image of her boyfriend being swallowed by the beast was burned into her memory, a nightmare she couldn't escape.

Minutes felt like hours, but finally, the sound of sirens broke through the tension. A couple of police officers arrived, their expressions serious as they approached the shaken group. The girlfriend ran to them, her relief palpable.

"Please, you have to believe me," she begged. "It's real. It killed him."

One of the officers, a tall woman with a no-nonsense demeanour, nodded. "We believe you. Show us where it happened."

The girlfriend led them back towards the lake, her steps faltering as they neared the spot. The Kelpie was gone, but the remnants of their picnic were scattered, a stark reminder of the terror that had unfolded.

The officer knelt and examined the area, her eyes narrowing as she noticed the unusual marks on the ground, signs of a struggle, and the strange, wet hoofprints that seemed to lead away from the scene.

"What could have done this?" the other officer muttered, more to himself than anyone else.

"I don't know," the first officer replied, standing up. "But we need to get more people out here to search the area. Whatever it was, it's dangerous."

As they radioed for backup, the girlfriend sank to her knees, her body shaking with sobs. She felt a hand on her shoulder and looked up to see the older man from before, his expression kind but troubled.

"You did the right thing," he said gently. "You got help. We'll find out what happened."

But as the minutes stretched into an hour, and more police arrived to comb the park, the reality of the situation began to sink in. The Kelpie was gone, vanished as mysteriously as it had appeared. The police found the boyfriend's phone, still recording, and the footage provided a chilling glimpse of the creature. But without any trace of the kelpie itself, it was hard to convince everyone of the truth.

The girlfriend watched as the officers discussed their next steps, feeling a mix of grief and frustration. She knew what she had seen, what she had experienced. But it all seemed so surreal, like a twisted dream she couldn't wake from.

Finally, one of the officers approached her. "We're going to continue searching the park," he said. "In the meantime, we'll need you to come with us and give a statement. We'll do everything we can to find out what happened."

She nodded numbly, allowing herself to be led away. As they walked, she glanced back at the lake, the spot where their peaceful afternoon had turned into a nightmare. She knew her life would never be the same, that the memory of the kelpie would haunt her forever.

In the days that followed, the story of the mysterious creature spread, capturing the public's imagination. Some believed her tale, others dismissed it as a figment of a traumatized mind. But those who had seen the footage knew there was something more to it, something that couldn't be easily explained.

The girlfriend stayed with friends, trying to piece her life back together. She avoided the park, the memories too painful to face. But every so often, she found herself drawn to the window, staring out at the world beyond, wondering if the kelpie was still out there, lurking in the shadows, waiting for its next victim.

The police continued their investigation, but as the days turned into weeks, leads dried up, and the case grew cold. The park returned to its usual tranquillity, the horrific events fading into the realm of urban legend.

As the minutes stretched into what felt like hours, the girlfriend clung to the strangers around her, their faces blurring as her mind raced. The police had arrived, their authoritative presence bringing a small sense of security. Yet, the horror she had witnessed left her feeling vulnerable and on edge.

"Please, you have to find it," she pleaded with the officers, her voice raw with desperation. "It's out there somewhere, it's dangerous!"

The tall officer, who had introduced herself, nodded firmly. "We believe you. We're doing everything we can. But we need you to stay calm and help us. Can you do that?"

She swallowed hard, nodding despite the tears streaming down her face. "I'll try."

The officer glanced at her partner. "get the rest of the team to secure the perimeter. We need to make sure no one else is in danger."

As Officer moved to carry out her orders, the tall officer turned back to the girlfriend. "Can you tell me exactly what you saw? Every detail could help us."

She took a shaky breath, trying to gather her thoughts. "It came out of nowhere… a portal or something. It looked like a horse, but not… its eyes were glowing, and it was dripping water. My boyfriend tried to take a picture, and it… it…"

Her voice broke, and an officer placed a reassuring hand on her shoulder. "It's okay. You're doing great. What happened next?"

"It attacked him," she whispered, her voice trembling. "It bit him and… swallowed him. There was nothing I could do. I just ran."

The tall officer nodded, her expression grim. "You did the right thing. You got help. We're going to find this thing, I promise."

Suddenly, a loud crackling noise came from their radios. "officer, We've found something. Over by the lake."

The tall officer squeezed the girlfriend's shoulder once more before stepping aside to respond. "What is it?"

"Not sure. You need to see this. It's… strange."

"What did you find….?" The tall officer asked as they approached.

pointed to the ground. "Look at these prints, the second officer said. They're wet, but there's no water source nearby. And they're unlike anything I've ever seen."

Just then, a commotion erupted from the far side of the lake. Shouts and the sound of running feet pierced the air.

One of the officers skidded to a halt, breathless. "We saw it! The creature! It's real!"

"What do we do?" she whispered.

The kelpie stood at the water's edge, its body half-submerged. It watched them with an unsettling calm, its eyes reflecting the light like two burning embers.

"Hold your positions!" the tall officer commanded. "We've got it!"

But the kelpie was not so easily subdued. With a final, desperate surge, it lunged towards them, its eyes blazing with fury. The girlfriend screamed, ducking behind the officer as the creature bore down on them.

"Fire again!" the tall officer yelled yelled.

In another part of London, the bustling city life continued unabated, unaware of the extraordinary events unfolding in the quiet corners of its parks and arenas. Near an outdoor college sports arena, the air shimmered briefly, unnoticed by the few people left in the vicinity. The last game of Jugglebubble had ended hours ago, and the only sounds were the distant hum of traffic and the occasional chirp of birds settling down for the night.

A janitor made his way across the field, his movements methodical and unhurried. He had a routine, one that he had followed for years, ensuring the grounds were clean and ready for the next day's activities. Retrieving softballs from the field after a game was a simple task, but one he took pride in. He had seen many games, watched as students competed and cheered, and enjoyed the quiet satisfaction of his work.

As he bent down to pick up a stray ball near the edge of the field, a faint glow caught his eye. He straightened up, squinting into the twilight, and saw something unusual near the portal that was often used for equipment storage. It was a ball, but not like any he had seen before. It glowed with a soft, ethereal light, hovering just above the ground.

Curiosity piqued, he walked over to the glowing ball, his broom dragging behind him. "What in the world is this?" he muttered to himself, reaching out tentatively. As his fingers brushed the surface, the ball ceased its glow, becoming an ordinary softball in an instant. He blinked, bewildered.

"Huh," he said, picking it up and turning it over in his hands. "Must be some new kind of ball the kids are using. Maybe it's one of those fancy glow-in-the-dark ones."

Shaking his head, he added the ball to his collection in the cart, stacking it among the other softballs. He resumed his task, but the strange encounter lingered in his mind. Every so often, he glanced back at the cart, half-expecting the ball to start glowing again.

As he continued his rounds, the field gradually grew darker, the overhead lights casting long shadows. The janitor hummed a tune under his breath, trying to shake off the uneasy feeling that had settled over him. He had always been a practical man, not given to flights of fancy, but the glowing ball was something he couldn't easily dismiss.

He finished collecting the last of the balls and began wheeling the cart towards the storage shed. The rhythmic squeak of the wheels was the only sound accompanying him. As he approached the shed, he heard a faint rustling noise. He paused, looking around.

"Who's there?" he called out, his voice echoing in the empty field.

Silence. He waited a moment longer, then shrugged and continued on his way. But the rustling resumed, louder this time, and he felt a prickle of unease. He turned back to the cart, peering at the pile of softballs. They seemed ordinary enough, but something felt off.

With a sigh, he set the cart down and carefully lifted the glowing ball from the pile. Holding it up to the light, he examined it closely. It felt like a regular softball, but the memory of its glow nagged at him. "What are you?" he murmured as if expecting the ball to answer.

A sudden, soft pulse of light emanated from the ball, startling him. He nearly dropped it but managed to catch it just in time. His heart raced as the ball began to glow faintly once more, a steady, rhythmic pulse like a heartbeat.

"What the...?" He stared in awe, unsure of what to do next.

Just then, a voice broke the silence. "Hey, everything alright over there?"

The janitor looked up to see a security guard approaching, flashlight in hand. He quickly tucked the glowing ball behind his back, not wanting to draw attention to the strange occurrence. "Yeah, everything's fine," he said, forcing a casual tone.

"Just finishing up."

The guard nodded, shining his light around the area. "Saw the lights still on and thought I'd check in. Don't usually see anyone around this late."

"Just me," the janitor replied with a tight smile. "Wrapping up for the night."

The guard gave a final sweep with his flashlight and then nodded again. "Alright then. Have a good night."

"You too," the janitor said, watching the guard walk away. Once he was sure he was alone again, he brought the glowing ball back into view. The pulsing light seemed to have grown stronger, casting a soft glow over his hands.

"What am I supposed to do with you?" he wondered aloud. He had half a mind to toss it away, but something about the ball drew him in. It was as if it had a presence, a quiet insistence that he couldn't ignore.

With a sigh, he decided to take it with him. Maybe he could figure it out later. He carefully placed it back in the cart, making sure it was secure, and continued on his way to the storage shed. As he locked up for the night, he couldn't shake the feeling that he was being watched.

Back at his small office, the janitor set the glowing ball on his desk, staring at it for a long moment. The glow was mesmerizing, a steady rhythm that seemed almost alive. He reached out to touch it again, and as his fingers brushed the surface, he felt a faint warmth.

"What are you?" he whispered, more to himself than to the ball.

The glow intensified briefly, as if in response, and then dimmed again. The janitor shook his head, rubbing his eyes. Maybe he was just tired. Maybe it was all in his head.

He leaned back in his chair, staring at the ball. Memories of old stories and legends flitted through his mind, tales of magical objects and portals to other worlds. He had never put much stock in such things, but tonight, he found himself wondering.

As the night wore on, the janitor's curiosity grew. He couldn't just leave the ball alone. He had to know more. He rummaged through his desk drawers, finding an old magnifying glass. Holding it up to the ball, he examined it closely, looking for any clues.

The surface was smooth and unmarked, but as he peered through the magnifying glass, he noticed tiny, intricate patterns etched into the material. They were almost too small to see, but they seemed to form a delicate, swirling design.

"What in the world?" he muttered, tracing the patterns with his finger. The ball pulsed again, a warm, gentle light that seemed to respond to his touch.

He sat back, thinking. Maybe this wasn't just a fancy piece of sports equipment. Maybe it was something more. He pulled out his phone and snapped a few pictures, hoping to find someone who could help him understand what he had found.

The rest of the night passed in a blur. The janitor couldn't stop thinking about the ball, its mysterious glow, and the strange patterns. He hardly slept, his mind racing with questions and possibilities.

The next morning, he was back at the arena early, the glowing ball carefully tucked away in his bag. He kept an eye out for anyone who might be able to shed some light on the situation, but he didn't want to raise any suspicions. He went about his usual tasks, the ball's presence a constant distraction.

As he cleaned and tidied, he replayed the events of the previous night in his mind. The ball's glow, the security guard's interruption, the patterns etched into its surface. There had to be an explanation.

he found a quiet moment and pulled out his phone, scrolling through the pictures he had taken. He zoomed in on the patterns, trying to make sense of them. They looked almost like writing, but in a language he didn't recognize.

He decided to do some research. During his lunch break, he sat in the break room, hunched over his phone. He searched for anything that might match the patterns, any clue that could help him understand what he had found. Hours passed, but he found nothing.

Frustrated, he leaned back in his chair, staring at the ball. "What are you?" he asked again as if expecting an answer.

The ball remained silent, its glow steady and unchanging. The janitor sighed, feeling a mix of wonder and frustration. He didn't know what to do next, but he couldn't just ignore it.

He showed the pictures to a few trusted friends, but no one recognized the patterns. He scoured the internet, looking for any mention of similar objects or phenomena, but came up empty-handed.

CHAPTER THREE

CHAOS AT THE IN-LAWS

Marcus and Scarlette entered John and Sheryl's home. John, Scarlette's father, is a retired military officer in his late fifties, with a face of discipline and authority. His greying hair and sharp eyes reflect his no-nonsense approach to life.

Sheryl, Scarlette's mother, is a warm and nurturing woman in her mid-fifties. With kind eyes and a gentle smile, she serves as the peacemaker in the family, often mediating between John and Marcus.

As they entered, the warm aroma of dinner filled the air. Marcus, always the jokester, grinned widely, his eyes sparkling with mischief. Scarlette, on the other hand, wore a nervous smile, her hand tightly clutching Marcus's arm as if to remind him to behave.

"Hello, everyone!" Marcus called out, his voice cheerful.

John looked up from the table, his expression already hinting at disapproval. "Evening," he said curtly, his eyes narrowing slightly as he regarded Marcus.

Sheryl, ever the peacemaker, hurried over with a smile. "Welcome, you two! Dinner is just about ready. Make yourselves comfortable."

Scarlette led Marcus to the dining table, giving him a stern look. "Remember, please try to be serious tonight," she whispered.

Marcus nodded, though his grin never faltered.

"Got it, babe. Serious as a heart attack."

Scarlette sighed, knowing that was the best she could hope for.

They sat down, and the tension in the room was palpable. John eyed Marcus with suspicion, while Sheryl attempted to lighten the mood with pleasant small talk.

"So, Marcus, how's work going?" Sheryl asked, her tone friendly.

Marcus leaned back in his chair, a playful glint in his eye.

"Oh, it's going great! I just got a promotion. Now I'm officially the Chief Executive of Nonsense."

Scarlette's face flushed with embarrassment, and John rolled his eyes.

"Do you ever take anything seriously, Marcus?" he asked, his voice edged with irritation.

Marcus, sensing the discomfort, decided to steer the conversation towards safer waters. "Well, to be honest, I don't wanna be a liar but this dish is on fire!" he said, chuckling at his own rhyme.

No sooner had the words left his mouth than flames erupted from the serving dish in the center of the table. Sheryl screamed, John jumped up, and Scarlette's eyes widened in horror.

"Marcus!" Scarlette yelled, grabbing a nearby pitcher of water and dousing the flames.

"What the hell, Marcus?" John shouted, his face red with anger.

Marcus stared at the charred remnants of the dinner, bewildered. "I—I don't know what happened! I didn't mean for that to—"

Sheryl quickly intervened, trying to salvage the evening.

"It's alright, it's alright. Let's just clean this up and order some takeout."

As the dinner ended in disastrous commotion, the couple excused themselves, their departure a mix of awkward apologies and strained smiles.

On the way home, the car ride was filled with an uncomfortable silence. Marcus kept glancing at

Scarlette, who stared out the window, her face set in a tense frown.

Finally, Marcus couldn't take it anymore.

"Scarlette, I'm sorry. I don't know what's happening to me."

Scarlette turned to him, her eyes flashing with frustration. "You embarrassed me in front of my parents! My dad already doesn't like you, and now this?"

"I know, I know. But you have to believe me, I didn't do it on purpose!" Marcus gripped the steering wheel tightly.

"I think… I think something's wrong with me."

Scarlette's expression softened slightly. "What do you mean?"

Marcus sighed. "Ever since this afternoon, weird things have been happening. I say something that rhymes, and then it actually happens. Like with the fire tonight."

Scarlette bit her lip, considering his words. "You mean, you have some kind of… power?"

"I guess so," Marcus said, frustration and confusion evident in his voice. "But I don't know how to control it."

Scarlette sighed. "This is a lot to take in. But, Marcus, you need to figure this out. We can't have things going up in flames every time you make a joke."

"I know," Marcus replied. "And I'm sorry. I'll try to be more careful."

They drove in silence for a few more moments before Scarlette spoke again. "Maybe we should talk to Alex about this. He always had a way of figuring things out."

Marcus nodded. "Yeah, that sounds like a good idea. Let's catch up with him, just like old times."

The tension in the car eased slightly as they both remembered the good times they had shared with their friend. It felt like a step towards normalcy, a way to deal with the strange new reality they were facing.

The next evening, Marcus and Scarlette found themselves in a cozy café, waiting for Alex. The familiar setting brought a sense of comfort and nostalgia, reminding them of the simpler times before all the chaos.

Alex arrived, his usual laid-back demeanor and friendly smile instantly putting them at ease. "Hey, you two! Long time no see."

"Hey, Alex," Scarlette greeted him, smiling.

"Good to see you, man," Marcus added, though his smile was more strained.

They exchanged pleasantries, catching up on life and reminiscing about old times. Eventually, the conversation turned serious as Marcus explained the strange occurrences.

Alex listened intently, nodding thoughtfully. "So, you're saying you have some sort of rhyming power that makes things happen?"

"Exactly," Marcus said, relief evident in his voice. "And I have no idea how to control it."

Alex leaned back, considering the situation. "Well, that definitely sounds unique. Have you tried testing it? You know, to understand how it works?"

Marcus shook his head. "Not really. I've been too worried about causing more disasters."

"Maybe we can figure it out together," Alex suggested. "We can test it in a controlled environment, see if we can understand the rules of your power."

Scarlette nodded, her expression hopeful. "That sounds like a good idea. We need to figure this out."

The atmosphere in the college arena was electric as spectators filled the stands, eagerly anticipating the Jugglebubble game between The Forest Gate Fireballs and The Fearless Knights. The VIP booth, with its luxurious seats and lavish spread of food and drinks, provided the perfect vantage point for Alex and his guests to enjoy the game.

The anticipation was palpable as Marcus, Scarlette, and their families arrived at the college arena. The air was filled with the excited chatter of spectators and the occasional roar of fans from the stands. They were ushered into the VIP booth, a luxurious lounge area offering a perfect view of the Jugglebubble court below.

Marcus, Scarlette, and their families settled into their seats, the excitement palpable. Ryan, a star player for The Fearless Knights, was already on the court, warming up with his teammates.

"This is amazing," Marcus said, taking in the grandeur of the arena. "I've never seen a Jugglebubble game live before."

"Wow, this place is incredible!" Marcus exclaimed, looking around at the plush seating and array of food and drinks laid out.

Scarlette smiled, her nervousness from earlier easing slightly. "It's going to be a great game. Ryan's team is really strong this season."

Scarlette's parents, John and Sheryl, exchanged glances. While Sheryl smiled warmly, John still wore a look of scepticism.

"Yes, it certainly is," John said, his tone neutral but his eyes still scrutinizing Marcus.

Scarlette squeezed Marcus's hand, giving him an encouraging smile. "Let's just enjoy the game," she whispered.

They found their seats, and soon Alex and his family joined them. Alex greeted everyone with hugs and handshakes, his charisma instantly putting everyone at ease.

"It's great to see you all again," Alex said, his smile genuine. "I'm glad you could make it."

Marcus grinned. "Wouldn't miss it for the world. Can't wait to see Ryan in action!"

Scarlette echoed his sentiments, while her parents gave polite nods.

The game soon began, and the energy in the arena was electrifying. The referee's whistle and the players immediately sprang into action. The Fearless Knights and The Forest Gate Fireballs were evenly matched, their movements precise and coordinated as they juggled and passed the bubble-like balls with skill and agility.

Ryan, in particular, stood out with his impressive footwork and quick reflexes. He maneuvered through the opposing team with ease, earning cheers from the crowd every time he made a successful play.

"Ryan's on fire today!" Alex exclaimed, beaming with pride. "Look at him go!"

Marcus, caught up in the excitement, shouted, "Yeah, he's unstoppable!"

Scarlette shot Marcus a warning look, and he quickly realized his mistake, clamping his mouth shut before any unintended magic could occur.

As the game progressed, Marcus leaned closer to Alex. "Ryan's really good," he said, admiration clear in his voice.

Alex nodded, his eyes fixed on the court. "He's worked hard. This is his passion."

The first half of the game was intense, with both teams showcasing impressive moves and strategies.

As halftime approached, The Fearless Knights held a narrow lead. The teams retreated to their benches for a brief respite, and the arena buzzed with conversation and speculation.

In the VIP booth, the atmosphere was jubilant. Alex poured drinks for everyone, his smile never fading. "We've got this," he said confidently. "Ryan and his team are playing their hearts out."

Sheryl nodded, her eyes shining with pride. "They are. It's wonderful to see."

John, though still reserved, couldn't hide a small smile. "They're doing well. Ryan's a talented player."

Marcus, wanting to keep the positive momentum, leaned towards John. "I've been learning a lot about Jugglebubble. It's fascinating how much strategy and skill go into it."

John looked at Marcus, his expression softening slightly. "It's more than just athleticism. There's a lot of teamwork and quick thinking involved."

The conversation continued amicably, with Marcus making a conscious effort to engage John and show his serious side. Scarlette watched with relief and admiration, grateful for Marcus's efforts.

Sheryl turned to Scarlette and Marcus. "So, how have you two been? Any new adventures?"

Marcus chuckled. "You could say that. We've been working on... controlling some surprises."

John raised an eyebrow. "Surprises, you say?"

Scarlette nodded. "Yes, but we're managing it together. And Alex has been a great help."

John grunted, clearly still wary, but he didn't press further.

As the first half came to an end, the crowd's energy surged once more. Ryan made a spectacular play, scoring a crucial point for his team. The VIP booth erupted in cheers, with Alex beaming with pride.

"That's my boy!" Alex exclaimed, his voice full of joy.

Marcus caught up in the excitement, couldn't help but make a playful comment. "He's on fire tonight!"

Scarlette's eyes widened, and she quickly whispered, "Marcus, remember what we talked about..."

Marcus nodded, instantly serious. "Right, right. I got this."

The game continued to be a nail-biter, with The Fearless Knights maintaining a slim lead as the referee blew the whistle for the first half.

Alex, feeling the exhilaration from the game, decided to take a moment to grab some drinks from the private lounge area. As he made his way down the hallway, he noticed a strange flicker of light out of the corner of his eye.

Turning, he saw a purple, aardvark-like creature standing before him.

"What the...?" Alex muttered, taking a step back. The creature, with large, expressive eyes and a curious demeanour, took a cautious step forward.

"Greetings, Alex," the creature said in a surprisingly clear and gentle voice. "I am Ardy, sent from Vesta of Esmeria. I bring urgent news."

Alex's heart raced, memories of his past adventures flooding back. "Esmeria? But... how? Why are you here?"

Ardy nodded, sensing Alex's confusion. "I understand this must be a shock. I've come to warn you that your arch-nemesis, Ruok, has gained considerable power over the years. He is using his magic to open portals, sending creatures from other dimensions into your world. His ultimate goal is to cause chaos and confusion, eventually taking over this world."

Alex felt a chill run down his spine. "Ruok? But I thought... I thought I had seen the last of him. I have a family now, Ardy. That part of my life is over."

Ardy's eyes softened. "I know, Alex. But Esmeria needs you. Your world needs you.

Ruok has managed to block access to Esmeria from your world, but there's still hope."

Before Alex could respond, Ardy picked up a fire ant from the ground and popped it into his mouth. With a dramatic flourish, Ardy shot a small fireball into the air, startling Alex. "This is my special ability. And here," Ardy continued, producing an intricately designed stick with a silver handle attached to a glowing ball,

"is the riddle stick. It contains riddles, instructions, and clues to guide you in your quest."

Alex hesitated, staring at the glowing ball. "Ardy, I... I don't know if I can do this again. I had good memories travelling to other dimensions, but I can't risk my family's safety."

Ardy stepped closer, his voice earnest. "Please, Alex. We need your help. You and your friends are the only ones who can stop Ruok."

Just then, the door to the lounge opened, and Scarlette's dad, John walked in, looking for a drink. He stopped in his tracks, eyes wide as he saw Ardy. "What the—?"

In a panic, Alex tried to hide Ardy behind a table, but it was too late. John's eyes rolled back, and he fainted, collapsing to the floor.

"Oh no!" Alex exclaimed, rushing to John's side.

The commotion drew the attention of the rest of the family, who hurried into the room. Scarlette's mum,

Sheryl, Scarlette, and Marcus gasped at the sight of Ardy.

"What is going on?" Sheryl asked, her voice a mix of shock and curiosity.

Alex quickly explained the situation, his words tumbling out in a rush. "This is Ardy, from Esmeria. He came to warn us about Ruok. John... well, he fainted."

Scarlette knelt beside her father, trying to revive him while glancing warily at Ardy. "Ardy, is it? Why are you here?"

Ardy repeated his explanation, his voice calm and persuasive. As he spoke, John began to stir, opening his eyes groggily.

"Did I... did I just see a purple aardvark?" John muttered, rubbing his head.

Sheryl helped him to his feet. "Yes, John. This is Ardy, and apparently, we have a bigger problem on our hands."

The family listened intently as Ardy pleaded his case, explaining the dangers Ruok posed to both their world and Esmeria. Gradually, their initial shock turned into a reluctant acceptance.

"Okay," Marcus said, breaking the silence. "So, what do we do now?"

Ardy handed the riddle stick to Alex. "This will guide you. But first, you must gather your friends and prepare. Time is of the essence."

Before they could discuss further, an announcement echoed through the lounge, reminding everyone that the game was about to restart.

"We'll talk more about this later," Alex said, hiding the riddle stick. "Let's get back to the game for now."

They all returned to their seats, trying to process the new information while focusing on the game. The second half had begun, and Ryan's team was under immense pressure. The Forest Gate Fireballs had taken the lead, and The Fearless Knights were struggling to keep up.

Ryan, determined to turn the tide, pushed himself harder. His friend Jane, sitting in the crowd, noticed his struggle and called out, "You can do it, Ryan!"

Her encouragement seemed to give him a burst of energy. Ryan juggled one of the bubbles, which began to glow strangely. None of them knew that this was the magical ball from earlier, which the janitor had unknowingly placed among the regular ones.

As Ryan approached the goal, the glowing ball began to pulsate. Suddenly, a portal opened from within the ball. Ryan, caught off guard, stumbled and fell through the portal.

"Ryan!" Jane screamed, leaping from her seat and running towards the field.

Sebastian, thinking Ryan might pass the bubble to him, also ran into the portal just as it was closing. Jane, acting on instinct, dove into the portal after them.

The crowd fell silent, stunned by what they had just witnessed. Alex and his family, in the VIP booth, were equally shocked.

"We have to do something," Scarlette said, her voice urgent.

Alex nodded, his mind racing. "Ardy, do you know where that portal leads?"

Ardy looked grave. "I fear it may lead to one of Ruok's traps. We must follow them, but we'll need the riddle stick to guide us."

"Then let's go," Marcus said, his face set with determination. "We can't leave them in danger."

Gathering their courage, Alex and his family, along with Ardy, prepared to follow Ryan, Sebastian, and Jane into the unknown. The arena buzzed with confusion and concern as they made their way to the spot where the portal had opened.

"Everyone, stay close!" Alex shouted, trying to remain calm despite the rising panic.

Out of the shadows, vampire-like creatures emerged—Ruok's Toxic Vampires from Alex's past, now more vicious and terrifying than ever. Their eyes glowed red, and their elongated fangs gleamed in the dim light. With superhuman speed, they attacked, sending everyone into a frantic scramble for cover.

Scarlette's mother, Sheryl, let out a strangled cry as one of the vampires wrapped its grotesque, long tongue around her neck, slowly draining her energy. "Help!" she gasped, her strength fading rapidly.

"Hey ugly!" Alex yelled, grabbing a nearby lamp and swinging it with all his might. The lamp connected with the vampire's head, causing it to release Sheryl and shriek in pain.

Marcus and John grabbed chairs, using them to fend off the vampires. Scarlette and her mother ducked under a table, trying to stay out of harm's way. Ardy, sensing the danger, reached into his pouch and popped a few fire ants into his mouth. With a swift motion, he shot fireballs from his snout, hitting several vampires and causing them to retreat.

The battle was chaotic. Alex swung the lamp wildly, connecting with another vampire that had lunged at him. Marcus, displaying surprising agility, used a chair to block an attack and then delivered a powerful kick, sending the creature reeling. John, despite his age, showed remarkable courage, using a chair to knock back a vampire that had cornered Sheryl.

Ardy's fireballs provided much-needed light and kept the vampires at bay, but the creatures were relentless. One managed to knock the chair from Marcus's hands and pinned him against the wall. Just as it was about to strike, Alex came to the rescue, smashing the lamp over its head and pulling Marcus free.

"We need to get out of here!" Scarlette shouted, fear evident in her voice.

"Keep fighting!" Alex urged, his voice steady. "We can do this!"

With a final burst of strength, they managed to push the vampires back. Ardy unleashed a particularly powerful fireball, causing the remaining creatures to flee into the darkness. The room fell silent, save for the heavy breathing of the exhausted group.

The lights flickered back on, revealing the damage to the lounge. Furniture was overturned, and scorch marks from Ardy's fireballs marred the walls. Despite the chaos, everyone was unharmed.

Sheryl, still shaken, was helped to her feet by John. "Are you okay?" he asked, his voice filled with concern.

"I think so," she replied, rubbing her neck. "Thanks to Alex."

Alex nodded, his expression serious. "We need to find Ryan and the others. Ardy, any idea where that portal leads?"

Ardy shook his head. "I'm not sure, but we need to hurry. Every moment counts."

Alex led the group back to the arena. The game had halted, and the crowd was in disarray, still processing the strange events that had unfolded. Alex's heart pounded as he scanned the area, desperate to find his son.

"Ryan!" he called out, his voice echoing through the now-silent arena.

Helen, standing beside him, her face pale with worry, joined in. "Ryan! Where are you?"

The rest of the family spread out, searching every corner. Ardy stayed close, ready to assist if needed. The tension was palpable, each second feeling like an eternity.

CHAPTER FOUR

THE RIDDLE STICK

Alex gripped the riddle stick tightly, his eyes scanning the intricate carvings that decorated its surface. Suddenly, a section of the stick began to glow, revealing a cryptic message that seemed to be written in an ancient language. The glow intensified, capturing the attention of everyone around.

"Look at this," Alex said, his voice tinged with urgency. "There's something written here."

Helen, still clutching Alex's arm for support, peered at the glowing inscription. "What does it say?"

Alex read aloud, his voice steady despite the tension.

"Where shadows dance and whispers fade,

An iron giant in darkness laid,

A portal hidden, secrets spun,

In London town, your quest's begun."

Marcus furrowed his brow. "What does that even mean?"

Scarlette shook her head, frustration evident in her eyes. "An iron giant? Shadows dancing? This riddle makes no sense."

John, despite his scepticism, leaned in to examine the riddle stick. "It mentions London. That's our first clue."

Ardy nodded thoughtfully. "The abandoned train station in Esmeria was our first portal. Perhaps the iron giant refers to something similar."

Scarlette's eyes widened with realization. "The station! We need to go back to the train station in Esmeria."

Marcus looked at her, hope flickering in his eyes. "It's worth a shot. Let's head there."

The group quickly gathered their belongings, as they made their way to the abandoned train station, their hearts heavy with anticipation and dread. As they approached the once bustling station, now a shadow of its former self, their hopes were dashed. The station was in ruins, a mere shell of what it once was. Rubble and debris littered the ground, and the air was thick with the scent of decay.

Alex's shoulders slumped. "This place is a wreck. How are we supposed to find anything here?"

Scarlette sighed. "Let's look at the riddle stick again. Maybe there's something we missed."

Alex held up the stick, and once more, it began to glow. The inscription changed, the words shifting before their eyes.

"In a city vast, where secrets sleep,

A portal waits in shadows deep.

Through London streets, the path is spun,

Find the place where iron meets the sun."

John frowned. "Iron meets sun? What could that mean?"

Marcus scratched his head. "Iron and sun... Could it be referring to a specific place in London? Something to do with iron, like a monument or structure?"

Ardy nodded. "It could be. We need to think of places in London that fit that description."

Helen's eyes lit up. "What about the Tower of London? It's old, made of stone and iron, and it has a long history with secrets and shadows."

Alex considered this. "It's a possibility. But it might also be something more modern. We need to explore all our options."

Scarlette pulled out her phone, quickly searching for iron structures in London. "There are a few possibilities: the Tower Bridge, the Iron Bridge, and even some old railway stations that were built with iron. We should check them all."

Marcus looked determined. "Then that's what we'll do. We'll search every corner of London if we have to."

Arriving in London, Marcus, Scarlette and Alex were greeted by the bustling city, a stark contrast to the ruins of Esmeria. The noise, the people, the energy—it was almost overwhelming. But they had a mission, and nothing would deter them.

First, they headed to the Tower of London, their hearts pounding with anticipation. They scoured the grounds, looking for anything that might resemble a portal or a clue. Hours passed with no success.

"This place is huge," Marcus said, frustration evident in his voice. "We could be here for days and not find anything."

Scarlette nodded, wiping sweat from her brow. "Let's move on to the next location. We can't waste too much time in one place."

Next, they went to the Tower Bridge, hoping for a breakthrough. The towering iron structure was impressive, but it offered no clues. They examined every inch but found nothing that matched the description in the riddle.

Scarlette sighed. "This is hopeless. We're running out of options."

Alex clenched his fists. "We can't give up. We'll try the Iron Bridge next."

The Iron Bridge, though less famous, was another potential lead. They arrived, their spirits waning but their determination unbroken. As they searched, Scarlette noticed something unusual.

"Look at this," she said, pointing to a small, hidden inscription on the bridge's iron support. "It's the same language as on the riddle stick."

Alex examined the inscription closely.

"It says, 'Where shadows meet the light of dawn, a portal opens to worlds beyond.' This must be it."

Marcus nodded, his excitement barely contained.

"We need to wait until the portal reveals itself then."

Mr. Ransford stood at the front of the classroom, explaining the finer points of algebra to a room full of attentive students. The sun streamed through the windows. Suddenly, a faint shimmering appeared outside one of the windows. At first, it was barely noticeable, a mere distortion in the air. But within seconds, the shimmer expanded, forming a small, swirling portal.

Before anyone could react, tiny dragons began pouring through the portal. The creatures were no larger than a cat, with scales that shimmered like gems and eyes glowed with mischief. They darted into the classroom, flitting about in chaotic patterns. One of the dragons landed on a desk, knocking over a stack of papers, while another snatched a pencil from a student's hand and flew away.

The classroom erupted into chaos. Students screamed and ducked under their desks, trying to avoid the dragons. One of the dragons breathed a tiny jet of flame, setting a stack of books on fire. Another dragon bit a student's leg, causing him to yelp in pain and jump onto his desk. The dragons were everywhere, causing havoc and destruction.

"Everyone, stay calm!" Mr. Ransford shouted, but his voice was barely audible over the din. He grabbed a broom and started swatting at the dragons, trying to shoo them out of the classroom. But the dragons were too fast, darting out of the way and continuing their rampage.

One of the dragons swooped down and grabbed a student by the collar, lifting him a few feet off the ground before dropping him back onto his chair. Another dragon flew around the room, scattering papers and knocking over books.

The air was filled with, the sounds of flapping wings, crackling flames, and panicked screams.

As the chaos continued, the school's fire alarm went off, adding to the commotion. Students from other classrooms spilt into the hallways, only to be met with the sight of tiny dragons wreaking havoc. Teachers tried to regain control, but the dragons were relentless, darting through the air and causing more destruction.

Amid the chaos, Mr Ransford managed to catch one of the dragons by the tail.

The creature squirmed and thrashed, trying to free itself, but Mr Ransford held on tight. He made his way to the window and threw the dragon outside. It disappeared through the portal, which was now starting to shrink.

One by one, the dragons followed their captured comrade, retreating through the portal until the last one was gone. As the portal closed, the room fell silent, save for the sound of the fire alarm and the crackling of the burning books. Students and teachers alike stood in stunned silence, trying to process what had just happened.

Later that afternoon, Mr. Ransford found himself in the school's conference room, sitting across from the school board.

The members of the board looked equally perplexed and concerned. The head of the board adjusted her glasses and cleared her throat.

"Mr. Ransford," she began, "we need to understand what exactly happened this morning. Can you explain?"

Mr. Ransford took a deep breath, still reeling from the events. "It appears that a portal opened outside the classroom window, and these small dragons came through. They caused a lot of chaos before we managed to get them back through the portal."

One of the board members leaned forward. "Portals? Dragons? This sounds like something out of a fantasy novel.

How do you explain this?"

Mr. Ransford nodded, understanding their scepticism. "I know it sounds unbelievable, but I've seen things like this before. Certain individuals have a deeper understanding of these phenomena. I believe we need to call Alex."

The mention of Alex brought a murmur from the board members. The head of the board looked thoughtful. "Alex Knight? Your student many years ago who was famous in the news for battling otherworldly threats with his friends Marcus and

Scarlette? The Realm Defenders? How would he be able to help us?"

Mr. Ransford leaned in; his expression serious. "Alex has dealt with these kinds of events before. He understands how to handle portals and the creatures that come through them. If anyone can help us make sense of this and prevent it from happening again, it's him."

The board members exchanged glances, weighing the options. Finally, the head of the board nodded. "Very well, Mr. Ransford. We'll contact Alex and bring him in to assist us. In the meantime, we need to ensure the safety of our students and staff. We'll need to assess the damage and put measures in place to prevent further incidents."

One board member spoke up again. "What about the students who were injured? How do we explain this to their parents?"

Mr. Ransford sighed. "We'll need to be honest with them. We'll tell them that there was an unexpected incident involving creatures from another dimension and that we're taking steps to ensure it doesn't happen again. We'll offer support to any students who were affected and work to rebuild their trust."

The meeting continued for some time, with the board discussing various measures to improve security and communication. Mr. Ransford's mind, however, was already on Alex. He knew Alex would have the answers they needed, and he hoped they could uncover the truth behind the portal and the dragons together.

CHAPTER FIVE

THE EVIL HELL DEFENDERS

The high street alleyway in central London was bustling as usual. Shoppers moved about, unaware of the looming danger. Suddenly, a swirling portal opened, emitting an eerie glow. From it stepped out three figures, twisted and monstrous versions of the heroes Alex, Marcus, and Scarlette. They were Lexa, Sarcum, and Eltscar—the "Hell Defenders."

People initially mistook them for the real heroes, rushing up to them for autographs. One child, clutching a toy sword, approached Lexa, his eyes wide with admiration.

"Are you Alex Knight?" he asked, holding a piece of paper.

Lexa looked down, a cruel smile curling his lips. "Alex? Oh no, little one. I'm Lexa." He leaned in close, his eyes darkening, and the child recoiled, screaming as his monstrous features became apparent.

A woman nearby gasped, her eyes widening in horror. "What's happening to them?"

Sarcum chuckled darkly, his eyes glinting with malice. "What's happening? We're bringing a bit of fun to your dull little world."

A man in a business suit stepped forward, frowning. "This isn't funny. You're scaring people. Where are the real heroes?"

Eltscar laughed, her voice a chilling sound that sent shivers down spines. "The real heroes? Oh, they're around. But they're not here to save you."

Before anyone could react, Sarcum raised his hands, dark energy crackling between his fingers. "Let's have some fun, shall we?" he snarled, releasing the energy into the crowd.

People began to scream as the dark magic hit them, transforming them into grotesque mutants. Their bodies twisted and contorted, and they cried out in agony. The high street descended into chaos, with people fleeing in all directions, trying to escape the madness.

Eltscar laughed maniacally, her voice echoing through the alleyway. "Run, little humans! Run!" She waved her hands, and more dark magic spread, turning more citizens into hideous creatures. The mutants stumbled and crawled, adding to the panic.

A woman, clutching her transformed child, looked up at Lexa with tears in her eyes. "Please, stop this! Why are you doing this?"

Lexa tilted his head, feigning sympathy. "Why? Because we can. Because it's fun." She then flicked her wrist, sending the woman and her child flying backwards.

The Hell Defenders revelled in the chaos, laughing and joking morbidly as they watched the destruction unfold. Lexa turned to his companions, a gleam of satisfaction in his eyes. "This is just the beginning. Imagine what we can do once we find the real Alex and his pathetic friends."

Sarcum nodded, his eyes glowing with malice. "Yes, they won't stand a chance against us. This world will be ours."

As the trio continued their rampage, turning more citizens into mutants and spreading fear, the portal behind them shimmered again. This time, no new threats emerged, but the portal's presence was a stark reminder of the Hell Defenders' origins and the dark power they wielded.

During the chaos, a brave armed police officer tried to approach them, his weapon drawn. "Stop right there! You need to come with us!"

Eltscar sneered, raising her hand and enveloping the officer in a dark mist. "Oh, I don't think so. You should join the fun instead."

The officer's eyes widened in terror as his body began to transform, his screams merging with the cries of the other victims. The Hell Defenders watched with twisted delight, their laughter growing louder as the chaos spread.

Meanwhile, Mr Ransford was frantically dialling Alex's number. His hands trembled as he held the phone to his ear. After a few agonizing rings, Alex picked up.

"Mr. Ransford?" Alex's voice came through, tinged with concern.

"Alex, we need you at the British Library," Mr. Ransford said urgently. "Something terrible is happening, and it involves doppelgängers of you and your friends."

"Doppelgängers?" Alex echoed, his voice dropping. "We'll be there as soon as we can."

Minutes later, Alex, Marcus, and Scarlette arrived at the British Library. The air was thick with tension and anticipation. Mr. Ransford paced back and forth, his face pale and drawn.

"What's going on?" Alex asked, his expression grim as he approached Mr. Ransford.

"It's worse than we thought," Mr. Ransford began, glancing around nervously. "There are doppelgängers—exact replicas of you, Marcus, and Scarlette. They're wreaking havoc across London, and

I believe they're connected to the dimensional portals we've been researching."

"We don't have much time," Alex said, leading the group inside the library. "We need to find out how these portals are opening and how to stop them."

The group delved into the ancient books on dimensional portals. Dust swirled in the air as they pulled volumes from the shelves. Scarlette found a book titled "The Mysteries of the Multiverse" and began reading aloud, her voice steady but urgent.

"According to this," Scarlette read, "portals can be controlled with the right knowledge and artefacts. We need to find the origin of the riddle stick and understand its significance."

Marcus, flipping through another book, looked up. "And we need to find out where your son and his friends are. They might hold the key to solving this."

"Exactly," Alex said, nodding. I need my son, Ryan, I can't lose a child.

Scarlette continued to read from "The Mysteries of the Multiverse." "The riddle stick is said to be an ancient artefact that can open and close portals between dimensions. Its origins are shrouded in mystery, but it's believed to have been created by a powerful sorcerer."

To find my son early, this means we need to focus on the riddle stick for me to unlock the secret of where my son and his friends are. Alex reacted. Scarlette replied with her face concerned.

"Yes," Marcus muttered. "So, we're dealing with ancient sorcery now. What do the riddles mean?"

Scarlette flipped through the pages, her eyes scanning the text. "The riddles are supposed to be clues—each one leads to the next, eventually revealing the location of the riddle stick's power source."

As they read, the library around them began to change. The wildlife section transformed into a dense jungle, with vines hanging from the ceiling and exotic birds flying past. The gang looked around in awe and fear.

"This is incredible," Scarlette whispered, her eyes wide. "It's like the library is coming alive."

But the transformation soon turned dangerous. The bookshelves morphed into cliffs, and the gang found themselves hanging onto the edges, trying not to fall.

"Hold on!" Alex shouted, reaching out to Scarlette as she struggled to maintain her grip. "We need to stay together!"

One by one, they lost their grip and fell into different sections of the library, now transformed into different mythical lands. Alex landed in a medieval village, its cobblestone streets winding through clusters of thatched-roof houses. He stumbled to his feet, trying to find his bearings.

"Scarlette! Marcus!" Alex called out, but there was no response. "We need to regroup," he muttered to himself. "We can't let the Hell Defenders win."

Marcus, navigating an enchanted forest, encountered magical creatures that both helped and hindered him. A unicorn blocked his path, its horn glowing with an eerie light.

"This is insane," Marcus said, pushing through the underbrush. "We need to find each other and figure this out."

Meanwhile, Scarlette found herself in an underwater kingdom, surrounded by mermaids and sea creatures. Her voice echoed through the water as she called out, "Alex! Marcus! Where are you?"

Eventually, they managed to escape the transformed library and met back at the entrance. Their relief was short-lived, however, as outside, the police were waiting, guns drawn.

"Freeze!" one of the officers shouted. "You're under arrest for causing the chaos in London!"

"Wait, you don't understand," Alex pleaded, holding his hands up. "It wasn't us. There are doppelgängers—evil versions of us—causing the destruction."

The officers exchanged sceptical glances. "That's a hard story to believe," one of them said, his grip tightening on his weapon.

Mr. Ransford stepped forward, his expression serious. "It's true. I've seen them with my own eyes. These are the real Alex, Marcus, and Scarlette. The ones causing the havoc are their evil counterparts."

The head officer hesitated, "Alright, we'll give you the benefit of the doubt for now. But we're going to the station together.

As the police lowered their weapons, Alex turned to his friends. "We need to stop the Hell Defenders and close these portals for good but eh….

Days later, Alex, Marcus, and Scarlette found themselves standing in a dimly lit courtroom, the weight of their predicament pressing down on them like a physical burden. The room buzzed with murmurs and whispers as onlookers filled the gallery, eager to witness the trial of the accused instigators of London's chaos.

The judge, a stern-looking woman with piercing eyes, rapped her gavel to silence the crowd. "Order in the court," she commanded. "We are here today to determine the guilt or innocence of Alex, Marcus, and Scarlette, who stand accused of causing widespread destruction and chaos in London."

Alex stepped forward, his voice steady but laced with desperation. "Your Honor, we did not cause the havoc. There are doppelgängers—evil versions of us—who are responsible for the destruction. We're being framed."

The judge raised an eyebrow, her expression sceptical. "Doppelgängers, you say? That is a difficult story to believe, Mr. Alex. Do you have any proof to support this claim?"

Before Alex could respond, the prosecutor, a sharp-suited man with a smug expression, stood up. "Your Honor, if I may," he said, holding up a remote control. "We have video evidence that clearly shows the defendants committing these heinous acts."

He pressed a button, and a large screen on the wall flickered to life. The grainy footage showed Alex, Marcus, and Scarlette evil doppelgängers—wreaking havoc across London. Fires raged, and people fled in terror as the doppelgängers laughed and caused destruction.

Alex turned to the judge, his eyes wide with urgency. "Your Honor, you have to believe us. Those aren't us. They're our evil counterparts. We would never do something like this."

The judge's expression hardened. "This video evidence is quite damning, Mr. Alex. It clearly shows you and your friends causing the destruction."

Marcus stepped forward, his voice firm. "Your Honor, please. We've been trying to stop these doppelgängers ever since we discovered their existence. They're using some kind of dark magic to impersonate us."

The prosecutor sneered. "Dark magic? Doppelgängers? This all sounds like a convenient excuse. The evidence is clear. These individuals are guilty."

Scarlette, her eyes pleading, addressed the judge. "Your Honor, we're not asking you to take our word for it. Look deeper into the evidence. There must be something that proves we're telling the truth."

The judge sighed, rubbing her temples. "This is a court of law, not a place for fairy tales. The evidence presented shows you committing these crimes. Unless you have concrete proof to the contrary, I have no choice but to find you guilty."

Alex's heart sank. "Your Honor, please. Just give us more time. Let us prove our innocence. We're fighting to save our world from these evil versions of ourselves."

The judge shook her head. "I'm sorry, but the evidence is overwhelming. I hereby sentence Alex, Marcus, and Scarlette to—"

Before she could finish, the gallery erupted in cheers. The crowd, once supportive, had turned against them, convinced of their guilt. Shouts of "Lock them up!" and "Justice for London!" filled the air.

Alex turned to his friends, his voice barely above a whisper. "We can't give up. We have to find a way to prove our innocence."

As the bailiffs approached with handcuffs, Marcus nodded resolutely. "We'll find a way. We always do."

Scarlette took a deep breath, her eyes steely with determination. "Together, we'll get through this."

The judge banged her gavel again. "Order! I hereby sentence you to be held in custody until your trial date. Bailiffs, take them away."

Alex, Marcus, and Scarlette were led away in cuffs, their hearts heavy but their resolve unbroken. As they were escorted out of the courtroom, Alex glanced back at the judge. "We won't stop fighting for the truth, Your Honor. You'll see. We didn't do this."

The judge's expression remained stony, but there was a flicker of doubt in her eyes. "We'll see, Mr. Alex. We'll see."

The heavy wooden doors of the courtroom slammed shut behind them, the sound echoing through the hallway like a final, ominous note. Alex looked at Marcus and Scarlette, his voice low but fierce. "We need to find a way to contact Ryan and the others. They might have more information that can help us."

Marcus nodded. "We'll figure something out. We can't let these doppelgängers win."

Scarlette's eyes blazed with determination. "We'll prove our innocence. No matter what it takes."

As they were led through the cold, sterile hallways of the detention centre, Alex's mind raced. They had faced impossible odds before, and they had always come out on top. This time would be no different. They would find a way to clear their names, stop the Hell Defenders, and save their world.

They were placed in a holding cell, the door clanging shut behind them. The cell was small and bare, with a single bench and a barred window high on the wall. Alex sat down heavily, running a hand through his hair. "We need a plan."

Marcus leaned against the wall, his arms crossed.

Scarlette paced the small space, her mind working rapidly. "There has to be a way. Maybe we can send a message through one of the guards. Or find a way to get a phone."

Alex nodded. "We'll figure it out. We always do."

As they settled into the cell, their minds focused on the task ahead, they knew that the road to proving their innocence would be long and difficult. But they were ready. They would fight with everything they had for their freedom, their loved ones, and the truth.

Lexa, Sarcum, and Eltscar, the evil doppelgängers known as the Hell Defenders, arrived at Alex's Mum's house under the cover of nightfall. As they approached the quaint suburban home, the air was thick with malevolence, shadows dancing ominously under the moonlit sky.

Alex's Mum, a kind-hearted woman with a gentle smile, was in the kitchen preparing dinner when she heard a knock at the door. She hesitated for a moment, a sense of unease prickling at her senses. She opened the door cautiously, her heart skipping a beat when she saw three figures standing on her doorstep, their faces twisted into monstrous masks of malice.

"Son! Marcus? Scarlette? Why do you look like…. monsters? What happened?

"Can I help you?" she asked, her voice trembling slightly.

Lexa, the leader of the trio, smirked darkly. "Oh, you can help us, all right," he said, his voice dripping with venomous charm.

Before Alex's Mum could react, Sarcum and Eltscar stepped forward, their eyes glowing with an unnatural light. Dark tendrils of magic snaked through the air, wrapping around Alex's mum, and immobilizing her with fear.

"No!" she cried out, struggling against the magical bonds. "Get away from me!"

Lexa raised his hand, a sinister grin spreading across his face. "Oh, we're not going anywhere," he said softly. "We're going to have a little fun with you."

With a flick of his wrist, Lexa unleashed a surge of dark energy. Alex's Mum cried out in pain as the magic coursed through her, transforming her on a fundamental level. Her screams echoed through the quiet neighbourhood, mingling with the unnatural sounds of her changing form.

Unable to bear witness to the horror unfolding, Alex's Mum collapsed to the floor, unconscious. The room fell silent, save for the crackling of residual magic and the ragged breaths of the Hell Defenders.

Sarcum knelt beside her, his voice dripping with sadistic satisfaction. "Pathetic," he sneered, his eyes glinting with cruelty. "She never stood a chance against us."

Eltscar, the silent enforcer of the group, stood watchfully nearby. Her gaze was cold and calculating, a testament to his unwavering loyalty to their malevolent cause.

Lexa surveyed their handiwork with a twisted sense of triumph. "This is just the beginning," she declared, her voice echoing with ominous certainty. "Soon, all of London will fall under our control."

As they prepared to leave, Lexa paused and glanced back at Alex's Mum's unconscious form. "Let this be a warning to you, Alex," he taunted, his voice carrying a chilling promise. "Cross us, and this fate will befall everyone you love."

With a final burst of dark magic, the Hell Defenders vanished into the night, leaving behind a trail of devastation and despair.

Mr. Ransford, Lucas, Alex's childhood bully from school now a changed person, Helen, and Ardy, the magical purple aardvark from Esmeria, approached the jail under the cover of darkness. Their faces were set with determination, knowing the gravity of their mission. The plan to break Alex, Marcus, and Scarlette out of prison had been meticulously crafted, and now, it was time to put it into action.

Ardy's magical abilities were unique and formidable. He could phase through walls, create illusions to distract guards and emit a soothing aura that could calm even the most panicked of minds. As they neared the jail's perimeter, Ardy's body began to shimmer with soft, purple light, signalling the activation of his powers.

"All right, everyone," Mr. Ransford whispered, his voice tense with urgency. "This is it. Ardy, you know what to do."

Ardy nodded, his large, expressive eyes showing both determination and a hint of nervousness. "Follow me closely," he said, his voice a gentle rumble. With a wave of his paw, he created an illusionary fog that enveloped them, masking their presence from the guards patrolling the area.

Lucas, who had once been Alex's childhood bully but had since become a loyal friend, felt his heart race as they approached the prison wall. "I never thought I'd be breaking into a jail," he muttered, his voice barely audible.

"But I know we're doing the right thing. Alex, Marcus, and Scarlette don't deserve to be locked up for something they didn't do."

Reaching the prison wall, Ardy phased through effortlessly, creating a shimmering portal for the others to pass through. They stepped into the dimly lit interior of the prison, the cold, sterile environment pressing in on them from all sides.

"Stay close," Mr. Ransford instructed. "We need to find their cell quickly."

They moved silently through the hallways, Ardy's calming aura keeping their nerves in check. Finally, they reached the holding cell where Alex, Marcus, and Scarlette were being kept.

Alex looked up as they approached, his eyes widening in disbelief. "Mr. Ransford? Lucas? What are you doing here?"

"Rescuing you, obviously," Lucas replied with a grin. "We saw what happened on the news. I know you're innocent."

Marcus stepped forward, gripping the bars of the cell. "Thank you. We need to get out of here and stop our doppelgängers. They're causing all this chaos." And to find Alex's son, Ryan and his friends.

Ardy's eyes glowed brighter as he focused his energy on the cell door. With a soft hum, the lock melted away, and the door swung open. "Quickly, we must leave before the guards notice."

They hurried out of the cell, moving swiftly through the corridors. As they approached the exit, Helen turned to Ardy. "Can you create another illusion to cover our escape?"

Ardy nodded, summoning a dense fog that filled the hallway, obscuring them from view. They slipped past the guards and out into the cool night air, their breaths coming in relieved gasps.

Outside the jail, Lucas took a deep breath, his expression earnest. "I couldn't just stand by and do nothing. When I saw the news and those doppelgängers, I knew it wasn't you. You've always been a good friend, Alex, and I had to help."

Alex clasped Lucas's shoulder, gratitude shining in his eyes. "Thank you, Lucas. Your belief in us means a lot."

Mr. Ransford stepped forward, his face serious. "We need to be on guard. These doppelgängers are dangerous. They're not just look-alikes; they possess dark magic and will stop at nothing to wreak havoc."

Suddenly, Alex's phone buzzed. He glanced at the screen and saw his mum's name. Answering quickly, he heard her panicked voice. "Alex! Those evil versions of you were here. They put some kind of dark magic on me. I don't know what to do!"

Alarmed, Alex replied urgently, "Hold on, Mum! I'm coming!" He turned to his friends; his face set with determination. "We need to get to my mum. She's in danger."

Mr Ransford nodded, leading them to his car. "Let's move. We don't have much time."

They piled into the car, the tension palpable as they sped through the streets. As they drove, Marcus turned to Alex, his voice filled with concern. "What did they do to her?"

Alex shook his head, worry etched into his features. "I don't know, but we'll find out. And we'll stop them. They've already caused too much damage."

Scarlette, sitting in the back seat, clenched her fists. "We'll protect her, Alex. Just like we've always protected each other."

As they neared Alex's home, Mr. Ransford spoke up, his tone grim. "Remember, we don't know what kind of traps they might have left behind. Be ready for anything."

The car screeched to a halt outside the house, and they quickly got out. Alex and his wife Helen led the way, bursting through the front door to find his mum sitting on the couch, her face pale and her hands trembling.

"Mum!" Alex rushed to her side, wrapping his arms around her. "Are you okay? What happened?"

She looked up at him, her eyes filled with fear and exhaustion. "Alex, they came… the evil versions of you. They did something to me. I feel so weak, like something is draining my life force."

Mr. Ransford knelt beside her, examining the faint, dark aura surrounding her. "It's dark magic, alright. We need to counter it quickly."

Alex hugged her tightly, We'll stop them."

Lucas, standing nearby, looked at the reunited family with a mix of determination and hope. "We'll all stop them. Together."

"We have a lot to plan," Mr. Ransford said, his voice steady. "But we can do this. We've faced impossible odds before, and we've come out stronger. This time will be no different."

Suddenly, the riddle stick, which Scarlette had been holding, began to glow with an intense light. The gang stared in awe as the light coalesced into a shimmering, translucent figure.

The figure spoke in a resonant, otherworldly voice. "Alex, son of Esmeria, hear me. I am the essence of the riddle stick. Your son, Ryan, and his friends are safe but held captive. Ruok has captured them to lure you into danger as revenge for conquering him many years ago when you were a teen."

CHAPTER SIX

THE EVIL PORTALS

Alex's heart skipped a beat. "Ryan… he's in danger because of me. Where is Ruok? What does he want?"

The figure continued, "Ruok is opening portals and allowing creatures from other universes to enter London. His actions have disrupted the natural flow of dimensional portals, causing other portals to open randomly. He is hiding in his world but is using ancient metallic silver ticks with small red jewels on their backs to drain energy from inter-dimensional beings, which keeps him strong."

Marcus clenched his fists, his anger rising. "So, we have to destroy these ticks to weaken Ruok and stop him from becoming invincible."

The figure nodded. "Yes. The dimensions where the ticks are will lead you to find your son. You must destroy all the ticks before Ruok drains enough energy to become invincible and rule over all dimensions. Once a task is completed in a dimension, a portal will naturally open, leading you closer to your destiny. This is how some dimensional portals work—they are complex and interconnected."

Scarlette asked, "But what about Esmeria? Can Vesta help us?"

The figure's light dimmed slightly. "Ruok has blocked the path to Esmeria. Even Vesta cannot intervene. You must do this on your own. However, once Ruok is destroyed, all those who have succumbed to the mutation will be restored to their normal state."

Alex's mum, still weak but more coherent, placed a hand on Alex's arm. "You have to go, Alex. You have to save Ryan and stop this madness. I'll be alright."

Helen, Lucas, and Mr. Ransford stepped forward, their faces determined. "We'll take care of her, Alex," Helen said firmly. "You focus on what you need to do."

Lucas nodded, his eyes fierce with resolve. "We'll protect her with our lives."

Ardy stood tall, his purple fur shimmering. "I will stand guard as well. No harm will come to her while you're away."

Alex looked at his friends and family, his heart swelling with gratitude and determination. "Thank you, all of you. We'll stop Ruok. We'll save Ryan. We'll make things right."

Mr. Ransford placed a reassuring hand on Alex's shoulder. "We believe in you, Alex. Now go, before it's too late."

As they stepped outside, the night air felt heavy with anticipation. The stars above seemed to twinkle with a sense of purpose, guiding them on their path. They knew that the journey ahead would be fraught with danger, but they were ready to face it together.

"Alright," Alex said, taking a deep breath. "Let's get moving. We have ticks to destroy and a son to save."

They piled into Mr. Ransford's car once more, the engine roaring to life as they sped off into the night, their hearts set on the mission ahead. The road to their destiny was uncertain, but with each other's support, they knew they could overcome any obstacle.

As they sped through the city streets, the riddle stick glowed with a pulsating light. Its voice echoed in the car, guiding them towards their next destination.

"Drive to London Bridge," it intoned. "There is an invisible portal waiting for you there. It will lead you to the first dimension where you must begin your quest."

Alex gripped the steering wheel, his knuckles white with tension. "London Bridge got it," he said, glancing at his friends. "Hold on, everyone. This might get rough."

As they neared London Bridge, the atmosphere grew tense. The city lights flickered ominously, casting eerie shadows on the road ahead. Suddenly, a black car that resembled a hearse roared up beside them. Lexa, Alex's evil doppelgänger, was at the wheel, his smile wicked and eyes glinting with malice.

"Looks like we've got company," Marcus muttered, his eyes fixed on the hearse. "They're trying to run us off the road."

Lexa's car swerved violently, sideswiping their vehicle and causing it to lurch dangerously close to the edge of the bridge. The Thames River glistened menacingly below, the dark waters churning.

"Hold on!" Alex shouted, trying to regain control of the car. "They're trying to knock us into the river!"

Scarlette clung to her seat, her face pale but determined. "We need to find that portal! Where is it?"

As if in response, the riddle stick glowed brighter. "The portal is near. Stay on course. Do not falter."

The hearse rammed into them again, harder this time. The gang was thrown against their seats as the car skidded dangerously close to the edge.

Lexa laughed maniacally; his eyes gleaming with malevolent glee. "You can't escape us, Alex! We'll drive you into the depths of the Thames!"

"We need to Stay focused, Alex. The portal is closed. We just need to hold on a little longer."

With another violent swerve, the hearse rammed into them, but this time, the riddle stick emitted a powerful burst of light. The world around them seemed to warp and twist, the bridge and the river blurring into a swirling vortex.

"Hold on!" Alex shouted as they were sucked into the portal. The sensation was dizzying, like being pulled through a whirlpool. The roar of the wind filled their ears, and for a moment, everything went black.

When they emerged on the other side, the car skidded to a halt on a strange, otherworldly landscape. The sky was a deep, unnatural shade of purple, with strange, luminous plants glowing all around them.

"Where are we?" Marcus asked, looking around in awe and confusion.

Scarlette checked the riddle stick, which now glowed with a steady, reassuring light. "We've made it to the first dimension. This is where we begin our quest."

Alex took a deep breath, his heart still racing from the encounter on the bridge. "Alright, everyone. We made it through the portal. Now we need to find those ticks and stop Ruok."

As Alex, Marcus, and Scarlette emerged from the portal, they found themselves in an astonishing landscape that was unlike anything they had ever seen before. The sky, a deep and melancholy shade of grey, seemed to weep, with droplets forming ethereal, misty rivers that flowed through the city. This place was alive with emotion, where feelings took physical form and created a surreal and magical world.

They stepped out of the car cautiously, their senses overwhelmed by the strange beauty and palpable sadness of the city. Buildings appeared to be made of shimmering tears, glistening in the dim light, and the streets were paved with the residue of countless emotions.

"Is this... the City of Tears?" Marcus asked, his voice hushed with awe and curiosity.

Scarlette nodded, consulting the riddle stick which now shone with a sombre, yet steady light. "Yes, it must be. The emotions here are so strong, you can almost feel them."

Alex took a deep breath, feeling a wave of melancholy wash over him. "We need to be careful. If emotions take physical form here, then our feelings could manifest in unpredictable ways."

As they moved, they noticed that the rivers of tears flowed with different intensities, some gentle and soothing, while others were torrential and chaotic. Clouds of sorrow drifted overhead, occasionally releasing bursts of rain that felt like pure despair.

Suddenly, a gust of wind whipped through the streets, carrying with it a sense of dread. The air grew thick, and out of the shadows emerged dark, ghostly figures.

These were the negative supernatural emotion beings – creatures born from the depths of fear, anger, and despair. Their forms shifted and twisted, reflecting the malevolent emotions they embodied.

"Stay close," Alex warned, his eyes scanning the surroundings for any sign of danger. "We can't let them touch us."

The gang moved cautiously, trying to avoid the creatures, but the beings seemed drawn to their presence. One particularly menacing figure, its eyes glowing with hatred, lunged towards them. Marcus reacted swiftly, using a makeshift he saw on the ground to fend it off.

"They're everywhere!" Scarlette exclaimed, her voice tinged with panic.

"We need to find the supernatural emotion of resilience," Alex said urgently. "It's the only way we can fight these things."

They continued through the city, their journey becoming increasingly perilous as more negative emotional beings appeared.

After what felt like an eternity, they arrived at a serene part of the city where the atmosphere was noticeably calmer. A gentle river of hope flowed here, its waters shimmering with a soothing light. At the centre of this peaceful oasis, a glowing figure stood – the embodiment of resilience.

"Look," Scarlette whispered, pointing towards the figure. "That must be it."

The being of resilience radiated a warm, comforting aura that seemed to repel the negative creatures. As they approached, the figure turned to them, its expression serene yet resolute.

"You have come seeking my strength," it said in a voice that echoed with unwavering confidence. "To fight the darkness, you must first embrace the light within yourselves."

The gang stood before the figure, feeling a surge of inner strength as its energy enveloped them. It was as if their fears and doubts were being washed away.

"We're ready," Alex said, his voice filled with conviction. "We need your help to battle the negative emotions and complete our quest."

The figure nodded, and a wave of resilience flowed into them, fortifying their spirits. "Use this gift wisely. It will protect you and give you the strength to overcome any obstacle."

As they absorbed the supernatural emotion of resilience, the gang felt a powerful transformation. Their senses sharpened, their courage intensified, and they knew they were ready to face whatever lay ahead.

Continuing their journey through the city, they soon encountered a scene that filled them with a mix of hope and dread. A metallic tick, grotesque and menacing, was latched onto a radiant creature of strength, feeding on its energy. The creature of strength struggled weakly, its light dimming with each passing moment.

"We have to help it!" Scarlette cried, rushing forward.

Alex and Marcus followed, their newfound resilience guiding their actions. They attacked the tick with all their might, using the strength they had gained to overpower the parasite. The tick writhed and screeched, but their combined efforts proved too much for it. With a final, desperate struggle, the tick was destroyed, disintegrating into a cloud of dark, foul smoke.

The creature of strength, now free from the tick's grasp, slowly regained its vitality. It stood before them, its luminous form glowing brighter than ever.

"Thank you," it said, its voice resonating with gratitude and power. "You have saved me from a fate worse than death."

The gang stood in awe as the creature of strength approached them, a look of deep appreciation in its eyes. "For your bravery and kindness, I bestow upon you a gift," it said, extending a shimmering, crystalline object towards them.

Alex took the gift, feeling its power pulse through his hands. "What is this?" he asked, marvelling at the object's beauty.

"This is the Crystal of Fortitude," the creature explained. "It will enhance your resilience and provide you with the strength to face even the greatest challenges. Use it wisely, for it will be a beacon of hope in your darkest hours."

With the Crystal of Fortitude in their possession, the gang felt an overwhelming sense of hope and determination. They had not only gained the supernatural emotion of resilience but also a powerful tool to aid them in their quest.

"Thank you," Alex said, his voice filled with gratitude. "We won't let you down."

The creature of strength nodded, its form beginning to fade as it returned to its domain. "Go forth with courage and resolve. Your journey is far from over, but you have the power to succeed."

As the gang continued their quest, With the Crystal of Fortitude and the supernatural emotion of resilience, they knew they had what it took to stop Ruok and save their world.

***

That night, London was gripped by fear. A citywide lockdown had been enforced, with the streets eerily silent except for the occasional siren wail. The news channels were ablaze with reports of the Investigation Force of Dimensions (IFD), a special unit tasked with maintaining order. However, there were darker whispers about the IFD's true mission – secretly kidnapping people affected by a mutant virus unleashed by the Hell Defenders.

In a modest living room, a group of concerned individuals huddled around a flickering television screen. Helen, Alex's mother Joanna Knight, Ardy, Lucas, and Mr. Ransford watched in horror as news anchors reported on the IFD's actions.

"This is madness," Helen said, her voice trembling. "They're breaking into people's homes and taking them away!"

Mr. Ransford nodded gravely. "They're not just enforcing the lockdown. They're hunting down anyone they think is infected."

Joanna's face was pale, her hands clenched tightly in her lap. "What if they come here? What if they take us?"

Ardy, a purple Ardvark-like creature, placed a reassuring hand on her shoulder. "We won't let that happen, Joanna. We'll hide you. They won't find you."

Lucas, tall and strong, stood up. "We need to act fast. The IFD is moving quickly. Joanna, we'll get you somewhere safe."

Before they could act, the sound of heavy boots and the clatter of a door being forced open echoed through the house. The IFD had arrived.

"Get down!" Lucas shouted, but it was too late. The front door burst open, and heavily armed agents stormed in, their faces obscured by dark helmets.

"Freeze!" one of the agents barked, his weapon trained on the group. "By order of the IFD, you are all under arrest!"

A fierce struggle ensued. Lucas lunged at the nearest agent, trying to disarm him, while Ardy and Mr. Ransford attempted to shield Joanna and Helen. Helen grabbed a nearby lamp and swung it at an agent, but her efforts were futile against their advanced gear.

"Stay back!" Helen screamed, but an agent struck her down with a stun weapon, electricity crackling through the air.

Mr. Ransford fought bravely, using a chair to fend off the attackers, but he too was overpowered, a stun weapon knocking him unconscious.

Lucas managed to tackle one agent to the ground, but another swiftly incapacitated him with a sharp blow to the back. Ardy, trying to protect Joanna, was similarly taken down, his body convulsing as the stun weapon's current surged through him.

Joanna screamed as the agents grabbed her, dragging her towards the door. "No! Let me go! Please, don't take me!"

Helen, struggling to remain conscious, reached out weakly. "Joanna…"

The last thing they saw before darkness claimed them was Joanna being forced into a waiting van, her pleas for help echoing in the night.

CHAPTER SEVEN

CITY OF EMOTIONS

Back in the City of Emotions, Alex, Marcus, and Scarlette were making their way through the strange, tear-filled streets. They had just received the Crystal of Fortitude and were feeling more hopeful about their mission. But as they moved, Alex began to feel a strange sensation.

"Are you alright, Alex?" Marcus asked, noticing his friend's pallor.

Alex shook his head, wincing. "I don't know. I feel… weak. Like something is draining my energy."

Scarlette looked worriedly at the riddle stick, which flickered with an ominous light. "Something's not right. The riddle stick should be guiding us, but it seems… confused."

The riddle stick then glowed brightly and spoke in a grave tone. "Beware, for the Hell Defenders have gone back in time. They aim to kill Alex and prevent your quest."

Marcus's eyes widened. "They're trying to kill you? But how?"

Alex's vision blurred, and he stumbled, barely catching himself. "I think… I think they've found a way to affect me here, across dimensions."

Scarlette grabbed Alex's arm, supporting him. "We need to get you out of here. The portal must be opening soon. We can't lose you, Alex."

The riddle stick shimmered again, indicating a portal nearby. "Your mission here is complete. Proceed to the portal to continue your quest."

With urgency in their steps, Marcus and Scarlette helped Alex towards the portal, battling the negative emotional beings that tried to impede their progress. The resilience they had gained gave them the strength to push through, their determination unwavering.

As they neared the portal, the city around them seemed to react violently. The rivers of tears surged, and the clouds of despair darkened. It was as if the city itself was trying to stop them.

"Almost there," Marcus encouraged, fending off a particularly vicious creature.

Scarlette tightened her grip on Alex. "Hold on, Alex. We're almost through."

With one final push, they reached the portal. The swirling vortex beckoned them, promising escape and a continuation of their quest.

"Let's go," Alex said weakly, but with determination. "We can't let them win."

Together, they stepped into the portal, leaving the City of Tears behind. The sensation of being pulled through dimensions was intense,

As Alex, Marcus, and Scarlette stepped out of the portal, the familiar sights and sounds of their hometown filled the air. They found themselves back where Alex was still a teenager discovering his powers.

Marcus glanced around, his brow furrowed in confusion. "Where's Alex? The younger Alex, I mean."

Scarlette, holding the riddle stick, looked around as well. "He must be at school. This is around the time he was learning to control his Ghost Coin powers."

Alex nodded, remembering the tumultuous days of his youth. "Yes, I remember this. I was still trying to understand my powers and not doing a very good job of hiding them."

The trio made their way to the school, a place filled with memories for Alex. As they walked through the gates, the familiar sights and sounds of school life surrounded them. They could see students bustling about, completely unaware of the extraordinary events unfolding around them.

"There," Marcus said, pointing towards a group of students gathered near a tree. "Is that him?"

Alex followed Marcus's gaze and saw his younger self, looking a bit dishevelled and nervous, holding the Ghost Coin. The younger Alex was attempting to practice his powers discreetly, but it was clear that he was struggling.

"Looks like he's having a tough time," Scarlette observed.

Alex smiled faintly. "I remember those days well. Trying to balance school life and these new powers was never easy."

They stayed hidden, watching from a distance as the younger Alex continued to experiment with his powers. It was a strange experience for Alex to see himself at that age, full of uncertainty and fear.

"Should we approach him?" Marcus asked.

Alex shook his head. "Not yet. He needs to learn on his own. Besides, we have other matters to attend to.

Leaving the school behind, the trio made their home. The familiar streets brought back a flood of memories for Alex, both good and bad. He entered the house quietly, and Alex found his stepfather, Paul, in the living room, looking agitated. The man looked up as he entered, his eyes narrowing in confusion and anger.

"What the hell is going on here?" his stepfather demanded, his voice rough with emotion. "Why do you look… older?"

Alex took a deep breath, struggling to keep his composure. "It's me, Alex. But not the Alex you know. I'm from the future."

His stepfather's eyes widened in disbelief. "What are you talking about? This is some kind of trick, isn't it?"

"No, it's not a trick," Alex replied, his voice trembling. "I know it's hard to believe, but I've travelled back in time. The Alex you know is at school right now, learning about his powers."

The older man shook his head, trying to make sense of the situation. "This is insane. You expect me to believe that you're from the future? Why are you here?"

Alex's eyes filled with tears as he looked at his stepfather, the man who had been both a source of conflict and a reluctant guardian. "I came to warn you. To try and change things. You… you don't have much time left."

His stepfather's expression softened, confusion giving way to concern. "What do you mean? What's going to happen?"

Alex swallowed hard, the words catching in his throat. "You're going to die. In the future, something terrible happens, and you won't make it. I wanted to see you one last time, to try and change your fate."

The room fell silent, the weight of Alex's words hanging heavily in the air. His stepfather sat down, his face pale and his hands trembling.

"How… how do you know this?" he asked, his voice barely above a whisper.

"Because I lived it," Alex replied, tears streaming down his face. "I saw you die. It broke me. I couldn't save you then, but maybe I can now."

His stepfather looked at him, a mixture of disbelief and sorrow in his eyes. "I've made a lot of mistakes, Alex. I haven't been the best father to you. But hearing this… it's a lot to take in."

Alex moved closer, reaching out to take his stepfather's hand. "I know you tried your best. I just want to make things right."

Marcus and Scarlette were crouched behind a row of lockers, their eyes darting around the hallway of the high school. They had been tracking the faint, flickering trails of Teen Alex's "Ghost Coin" invisible powers. The school was alive with the sounds of chatter and the occasional slam of locker doors, making their covert mission even more challenging.

Marcus pressed the button on his walkie-talkie, his voice a hushed whisper. "Alex, do you copy? We need you to get to the school ASAP. We're close to finding your past self, but we can't do it alone."

There was a brief crackle of static before Alex's voice came through. "I copy, Marcus. I'll be there soon." The tone of Alex's voice was strained. Scarlette, her eyes fixed on the corridor ahead, added, "Alex, we think Teen Alex is in the science wing. His powers have left some kind of residual energy. It's faint, but we're picking it up."

Alex's reply was immediate. "Understood. Heading your way now. Keep an eye on him and stay safe."

Back at his home, Alex took a deep breath, steeling himself for what lay ahead. He turned to his stepdad, who was watching him with a concerned expression. The weight of the moment and Alex's emotions were barely contained.

"I have to go now," Alex said, his voice trembling slightly. "I... I need to save someone very important. It was good to see you again, even if it was just for a short while."

His stepdad, clearly confused but sensing the gravity of Alex's words, shook his head. "I don't understand what's going on, but... be careful. And come back safe."

Alex hugged him tightly, tears welling up in his eyes. "I'll try. Thank you... for everything." With that, he pulled away and left, his heart heavy but his resolve firm.

As Alex made his way to the school, his mind raced with thoughts of the past and the significance of the mission. He couldn't afford to fail; the stakes were too high.

Meanwhile, Marcus and Scarlette continued their search, their movements synchronized and efficient. They scanned the area meticulously, their focus unwavering. Scarlette spotted a faint shimmer near one of the classrooms.

"Marcus, over here," she whispered urgently. "I think we've got something."

Marcus joined her, his eyes narrowing as he observed the subtle disturbance in the air. "Yeah, that's Teen Alex's power signature. He's close."

They moved closer, their senses on high alert. The tension was palpable, and the weight of their mission hung heavily in the air. Scarlette's walkie-talkie crackled to life again.

"Marcus, Scarlette, I'm at the school," Alex's voice came through, breathless but determined. "Where are you guys?"

"Science wing, near the second-floor classrooms," Marcus replied. "We're closing in on your past self. Hurry, Alex. We need you here."

Alex quickened his pace, his mind racing with a mixture of fear and hope. He navigated the familiar hallways, each step bringing him closer to a confrontation with his past.

As he rounded the corner, he spotted Marcus and Scarlette near a classroom door, their expressions tense but relieved at his arrival. Alex joined them, his heart pounding in his chest.

"Any sign of him?" Alex asked, his voice low.

Scarlette nodded. "He's in there. We need to be careful. His powers are unstable, and we don't know how he'll react."

Alex took a deep breath, steeling himself for the encounter. "Let's do this. We have to save him... and ourselves."

The gang finally found Teen Alex of the past in a quiet, dimly lit corner of the school corridor. The sight that greeted them made their blood run cold. Teen Alex was stuck to the wall, covered in a thick, viscous slime that pulsed with a sickly glow. His face was contorted in pain, and his body was trembling as the slime slowly drained him of his Ghost Coin powers.

Standing before him were their evil doppelgängers, the Hell Defenders, armed with slime-blaster weapons that emitted greenish light. Lexa, the leader of the Hell Defenders, turned to face them with a sneer.

"Well, well, well," Lexa said in an unearthly voice, his eyes glowing with malevolent delight. "I was wondering when you'd show up."

The Hell Defenders laughed in unison, their voices echoing with a sinister, otherworldly tone. They moved with a predatory grace, their eyes never leaving the gang.

"Let him go!" Alex shouted, stepping forward with a defiant glare. "This ends now!"

Lexa chuckled, his laugh sending shivers down their spines. "Oh, I don't think so. You see, we've been waiting for this moment for a long time. And now, we're going to finish what we started."

With a wicked grin, Lexa began to chant in a language that resonated with dark, arcane power. The Hell Defenders joined in, their voices blending into a haunting melody that seemed to vibrate through the very fabric of reality.

The air around them crackled with energy, and a portal began to form. From its swirling depths, a monstrous figure emerged a Chimera, a terrifying creature with the body of a lion, the head of a goat, and the tail of a serpent. Its eyes glowed with a malevolent intelligence, and it let out a bone-chilling roar.

The corridor erupted into chaos as the gang scattered, trying to evade the Chimera's ferocious attacks. Students poured out of classrooms, their screams filling the air as they fled in terror.

The Chimera's claws scraped against the tiled floor, sending sparks flying. It prowled forward, its three heads snapping and snarling, eyes fixed on its prey. Alex, Marcus, and Scarlette ducked into a classroom, slamming the door shut behind them. The sound of the Chimera's roar reverberated through the walls, a reminder of the danger lurking just outside.

"We need a plan!" Alex said, his voice hushed but urgent. He could hear the beast's heavy breathing and the scraping of its claws against the door. "We can't just hide forever."

The Chimera's claws tore through the wood, splintering the door. It was only a matter of time before it broke through. The gang looked around desperately for anything they could use to defend themselves.

"Over here!" Scarlette yelled, leading them into the science lab section of the classroom. They barricaded the door with desks and chairs, but it was a temporary measure at best. The Chimera's roars grew louder, more frenzied.

"Think, think!" Marcus muttered, his eyes darting around the room. "We need to slow it down!"

Scarlette grabbed a beaker filled with a bright green liquid. "What about this? It's some kind of chemical. Maybe it can help."

Alex nodded, grabbing a handful of beakers and throwing them at the door. The chemicals hissed and bubbled as they splashed onto the Chimera, causing it to roar in pain and fury. The creature stumbled, its movements becoming sluggish.

"It's working!" Marcus exclaimed, grabbing more chemicals and hurling them at the Chimera. The beast thrashed wildly, but the combined effects of the chemicals began to take their toll.

The Chimera backed away from the door, shaking its head violently as it tried to shake off the effects of the chemicals. Its eyes were filled with a murderous rage, and it lunged at the door again, smashing through the barricade. The gang scattered, diving behind lab tables and cabinets.

"Stay quiet," Alex whispered, his heart pounding in his chest. He could hear the Chimera sniffing the air, searching for them. The room was filled with the acrid smell of chemicals and the sounds of their ragged breathing.

The Chimera prowled through the lab, its heads turning this way and that as it hunted for its prey. Its lion's head let out a low growl, while the goat's head bleated eerily. The serpent's tail lashed out, knocking over equipment and shattering glass.

Scarlette peeked out from behind a table, her eyes wide with fear. She saw the Chimera's lion head sniffing the air, its eyes narrowing as it zeroed in on her hiding spot. She ducked back just in time as the beast lunged, its claws scraping against the floor where she had been moments before.

"We can't keep this up," Marcus whispered, his voice trembling. "We need to do something, fast."

Alex's eyes landed on a large container of a particularly volatile chemical. "Over there," he whispered, pointing. "If we can get that and throw it at the Chimera, it might just be enough to knock it out."

They moved cautiously, staying low and out of sight. The Chimera continued its hunt, its movements becoming more erratic as the chemicals took their toll.

Alex reached the container first, lifting it with a grunt of effort.

"Now!" he shouted, hurling the container at the Chimera. It shattered on impact, the chemicals reacting violently. The Chimera roared, thrashing wildly as the fumes enveloped it. It stumbled, its heads shaking as it tried to stay on its feet.

Marcus and Scarlette joined in, throwing whatever chemicals they could find at the beast. The room filled with a toxic haze, and the Chimera's movements grew more sluggish by the second. With a final, mighty roar, the Chimera collapsed, its eyes fluttering shut as it fell into a deep sleep.

The gang stood there, breathing heavily, watching the beast to make sure it was truly down. The classroom was a wreck, with glass and chemicals scattered everywhere.

we did Marcus shouted. "But we need to help Teen Alex."

They rushed back to the corridor where Teen Alex was still stuck to the wall, the slime continuing to drain his energy. Alex reached out, trying to peel the slime away, but it clung stubbornly to his younger self.

"Hold on, Alex," Marcus said, grabbing a nearby metal rod. "We'll get you out of this."

As they worked to free Teen Alex, he managed to summon a burst of energy, his eyes glowing with a ghostly light. With a fierce cry, he unleashed a ghostly force field that pushed the Hell Defenders back, pinning them against the walls.

"Hurry," Teen Alex urged, his voice strained but determined. "Run while you can."

Alex nodded, a mixture of pride and gratitude in his eyes. "Thank you, Alex. You're a hero."

Teen Alex managed a weak smile. "Hey! I still look good in the future."

Alex laughed, a genuine sound of relief and joy. "Thanks, Alex. Stay strong."

A portal began to open nearby, its swirling depths beckoning them. Just then, they spotted one of Ruok's ticks scuttling towards the portal, its dark form a stark contrast to the light.

"Hey! It's Ruok's tick!" Alex shouted, pointing at the creature. "It must have been hiding here! We have to destroy it!"

The gang didn't hesitate. They dashed towards the portal, their steps fueled by determination. Behind them, the Hell Defenders struggled against the force field, their eyes burning with rage.

"Go!" Teen Alex shouted, his energy faltering. "I'll hold them off as long as I can."

With one last look back, the gang leaped through the portal, the sensation of being pulled through dimensions washing over them. As they emerged on the other side, they found themselves in a new, unfamiliar landscape. The sky was a turbulent mix of colors, and the ground beneath them seemed to pulse with a strange energy.

"We made it," Marcus said, looking around. "But where are we?"

"We'll figure that out later," Scarlette replied, her eyes scanning the area. "First, we need to find that tick and destroy it."

Alex nodded, his resolve hardening. "Let's move. We can't let Ruok win."

As they set off in search of the tick, the Hell Defenders continued their struggle against Teen Alex's force field. Lexa's eyes blazed with fury as he watched the portal begin to close.

"This isn't over," he snarled, his voice echoing with unearthly power. "We will find you. And when we do, you'll wish you had never been born."

Teen Alex held his ground, his energy nearly spent. "Bring it on," he whispered, his voice filled with defiance. "We're ready for you."

The portal closed with a final flash of light, leaving the Hell Defenders trapped in their dimension. Teen Alex collapsed to the ground, exhausted but victorious. He had bought his future self and his friends the time they needed.

Meanwhile, in the new dimension, the gang moved cautiously through the strange landscape. The air was thick with tension, and every shadow seemed to hold potential danger.

"Stay alert," Marcus said, his eyes scanning their surroundings. "We don't know what else might be out here."

Scarlette nodded, her grip tightening on her weapon. "We need to find that tick and destroy it before it can do any more damage."

Alex's son, Ryan, Jane, and Sebastian found themselves in a dimly lit dungeon, the air thick with dampness and an unsettling chill. The walls were lined with jagged rocks, and the only light came from torches that flickered weakly, casting eerie shadows around them.

"How did we even get here?" Jane muttered, looking around with a mix of confusion and fear.

Sebastian shot a glare at Ryan. "We wouldn't be here if you had just passed me the bubble ball like you were supposed to!"

Ryan's face flushed with anger. "Are you serious, Sebastian? I was right near the goal! I was about to score! Why would I pass it to you?"

"Because you're not the only one on the team!" Sebastian snapped back, his voice rising. "You always think you have to do everything by yourself!"

Ryan clenched his fists, his frustration boiling over. "Oh, so now it's my fault we're trapped in this creepy dungeon? Give me a break!"

Jane, her patience wearing thin, stepped between them. "Enough! Both of you! This isn't helping. We need to focus on figuring out where we are and how to get out of here."

Ryan and Sebastian fell silent, their anger giving way to the realization of their predicament. Jane walked to the barred window and peered outside, her eyes widening at the sight.

"Guys, come look at this," she said, her voice tinged with awe.

Ryan and Sebastian joined her at the window, and their jaws dropped. The landscape outside was like nothing they had ever seen. The sky was a swirling canvas of colors, and the ground seemed to pulse with a rhythm that resonated through their bodies. Trees with musical notes for leaves swayed gently, producing a melody that filled the air.

"Where are we?" Ryan whispered, his anger forgotten as he stared at the otherworldly scene.

"I have no idea," Jane replied, shaking her head. "But we need to find a way out of here."

Sebastian turned away from the window, his expression grim. "We should call for help. Maybe someone will hear us."

They began shouting, their voices echoing off the stone walls. "Help! Is anyone there? Help us!"

Their cries were abruptly cut off by the sound of heavy footsteps. The door to their cell swung open, and a large, menacing ogre-like guard stormed in, his eyes blazing with anger.

"Shut up!" he bellowed, his voice shaking the walls. "Or I'll make sure you never speak again!"

The three of them backed away, retreating to the corner in fear. The guard's presence was overwhelming, and his threat hung in the air like a dark cloud.

"We're sorry," Jane stammered, her voice trembling. "We just… we just want to go home."

The guard snorted, a cruel smile curling on his lips. "Home? Do you think you can just leave? You're in the Dungeon of Harmonies now. No one leaves without permission from the Maestro."

"The Portal Master?" Ryan asked, his curiosity piqued despite his fear. "Who's that?"

The guard's smile widened. "You'll find out soon enough. For now, keep quiet if you value your lives."

With that, he turned and stomped out of the cell, slamming the door behind him. The sound echoed through the dungeon, leaving a heavy silence in its wake.

Jane sank to the floor, her mind racing. "We need a plan. We can't stay here and wait for something worse to happen."

Ryan nodded, his determination returning. "We have to figure out who their master is, and why we're here. Maybe then we can find a way out."

Sebastian sighed, rubbing his temples. "Fine. But let's not forget why we're in this mess in the first place."

"That doesn't matter now," Jane said firmly. "We have to work together to get out of here alive."

The three of them huddled together, their earlier argument forgotten as they tried to devise a plan. The melody from the trees outside drifted through the window, a haunting reminder of the strange world they were trapped in.

Hours seemed to pass as they sat in the dim light of the dungeon, each lost in their thoughts. Finally, Jane broke the silence.

"We need to find a way to communicate with someone outside this cell," she said. "Maybe we can use something in here to send a signal."

Ryan looked around, his eyes scanning the room. "What about the torches? We could use the fire to create smoke signals."

Sebastian frowned. "And risk burning ourselves alive? There has to be a better way."

Jane's eyes lit up as an idea struck her. "The music! The trees outside make music. Maybe if we can create a rhythm or a melody, someone will hear us and come to investigate."

Ryan nodded slowly. "It's worth a shot. But how do we make music in here?"

CHAPTER EIGHT

RESCUE

The night was eerily still as Lucas, Helen, Mr. Ransford, and Ardy gathered in a dark alleyway near the IDF headquarters. They had spent hours meticulously planning their mission, knowing that any mistake could cost them dearly.

Lucas adjusted his stolen guard uniform, his jaw set with determination. "Remember, we go in, get Joanna and the others, and get out. No unnecessary risks."

Helen nodded, her face pale but resolute. "We can't let them continue these experiments. It's inhumane."

Mr. Ransford, looking every bit the part of a grizzled veteran, checked his watch. "It's time. Let's move."

Ardy, the purple aardvark-like creature, twitched his snout and made a small noise of affirmation. "I've got my fire ants ready. Just give the word."

They approached the entrance to the IDF HQ, their hearts pounding. Lucas flashed their forged IDs to the guard at the gate, who barely glanced at them before waving them through. Inside, the fluorescent lights and sterile corridors contrasted sharply with the tension in the air.

As they walked, Helen whispered, "We need to find the lab where they're holding the infected. Any ideas?"

Lucas glanced at a map on the wall. "The sub-basement. That's where they keep the high-security experiments."

They made their way to the elevators, trying to act casual. As they descended, the sense of foreboding grew stronger. When the doors opened, they stepped into a dimly lit hallway. The sound of muffled cries and mechanical hums filled the air.

"Stay sharp," Mr. Ransford said, leading the way. "We need to be in and out quickly."

They followed the sounds to a large, reinforced door. Lucas pulled out a security card they had swiped from an unsuspecting guard earlier and swiped it through the reader. The door clicked open, revealing a horrifying scene inside.

Rows of metal tables lined the room, each holding a restrained individual with various mutations. Scientists in lab coats moved between them, discussing their findings in hushed tones. At the far end of the room, Joanna Knight lay on a table, her face contorted in pain.

Helen's breath caught in her throat. "Joanna!"

Before anyone could react, Lucas raised a finger to his lips, signalling for silence. "We need to do this quietly," he whispered.

They slipped into the room, blending in with the shadows. As they moved towards Joanna, they overheard snippets of conversations.

"We've made significant progress with the mutation serum," one scientist said. "If we can stabilize it, the military applications could be revolutionary."

Another replied, "The higher-ups are very interested. They see potential in using these mutants as biological weapons."

Helen's eyes blazed with anger. "We can't let this happen."

Lucas nodded, his expression grim. "Let's get them out of here."

They reached Joanna's table, and Helen gently shook her awake. "Joanna, it's us. We're getting you out."

Joanna's eyes fluttered open, a mix of relief and confusion crossing her face. "Helen? Lucas? How did you—?"

"No time to explain," Lucas said, working quickly to free her restraints. "We need to move."

As they freed Joanna, Mr. Ransford and Ardy moved to the other tables, quietly releasing the other prisoners. The alarm system remained silent, but Lucas knew it wouldn't last.

Just as they were about to make their escape, the inevitable happened. A scientist turned and saw them, his eyes widening in shock. "Intruders! Security!"

The alarm blared to life, red lights flashing throughout the lab. Armed guards poured into the room, weapons at the ready.

Ardy, his snout twitching with determination, reached into his pocket and pulled out a handful of fire ants. He gobbled them up, and his snout began to glow.

"Stand back!" Ardy shouted, shooting fireant fireballs at the guards. The flames erupted, causing chaos and confusion. The guards scrambled, trying to avoid the searing heat.

Lucas and Helen took the opportunity to lead Joanna and the others towards the exit. Mr. Ransford covered their retreat, using a makeshift shield to deflect incoming shots.

"Keep moving!" he yelled. "We don't have much time!"

They raced through the corridors, the sound of pursuit hot on their heels. Ardy continued to unleash fireballs, buying them precious seconds. The air was thick with smoke and the acrid smell of burning metal.

Finally, they burst through a side door and into the cool night air. Lucas scanned the area, spotting a van parked nearby.

"Over here!" he called, leading the group towards the vehicle.

They piled into the van, Lucas taking the wheel. He floored the gas pedal, the tires screeching as they sped away from the IDF headquarters. The sounds of alarms and gunfire faded into the distance.

As they drove, Helen tended to Joanna's injuries. "Are you okay?"

Joanna nodded weakly. "I am now, thanks to you."

Lucas glanced in the rearview mirror, his expression one of grim satisfaction. "We did it. But this isn't over. The IDF will come after us."

Mr. Ransford, his face set with determination, replied, "Let them. We'll be ready."

Ardy, still panting from his fiery exertions, nodded. "Next time, they'll regret crossing us."

They drove through the night, the weight of their victory tempered by the knowledge that the battle was far from won. But for now, they had saved Joanna and the others. And that was enough. ---

As they drove away from the IDF headquarters, the tension in the van was palpable. The city lights blurred past the windows as they sped through the darkened streets. Joanna leaned against Helen, her breathing still labored.

"How did you find me?" Joanna asked weakly, her eyes flickering open and closed.

Helen brushed a strand of hair from Joanna's face. "We never gave up looking. Lucas had a contact who gave us a tip about the IDF's secret operations."

Joanna's eyes widened slightly. "The experiments... they were trying to turn us into weapons."

Mr. Ransford, sitting in the front passenger seat, turned to look at Joanna. "We overheard. The IDF plans to use mutants in warfare. We couldn't let that happen."

Ardy, his snout still glowing faintly from the fire ants, chimed in, "And we won't. We'll find a way to stop them."

Lucas navigated the van through a series of narrow alleyways, trying to avoid any potential pursuit. "We need a safe place to regroup. Any ideas?"

Helen looked thoughtful. "There's an old warehouse on the outskirts of town. It used to be a safehouse for resistance members. It should still be secure."

Lucas nodded, adjusting his route. "Good. We'll head there."

As the van made its way towards the warehouse, the group sat in a tense silence. The reality of their situation was sinking in. They had made a daring escape, but they were far from safe.

When they finally reached the warehouse, Lucas parked the van and they quickly unloaded, helping Joanna and the other freed captives inside. The interior of the warehouse was dusty and filled with old, abandoned equipment, but it offered a semblance of safety.

Helen set Joanna down on a makeshift bed, checking her wounds. "We need to get you proper medical attention, but this will have to do for now."

Joanna grasped Helen's hand, her eyes filled with gratitude. "Thank you. I don't know what I would have done without you."

Helen smiled reassuringly. "We're a team. We look out for each other."

Lucas and Mr. Ransford secured the entrances, setting up makeshift barricades. Ardy kept watch near a window, his sharp eyes scanning the surroundings for any signs of danger.

"Lucas," Mr. Ransford said quietly, "we need to come up with a plan. The IDF won't rest until they find us."

Lucas nodded, his expression grim. "I know. We need to find a way to expose their operations. If we can get evidence to the public, maybe we can turn the tide."

Helen joined them, her face set with determination. "We also need to find a way to protect the mutants they've already captured. We can't leave them to suffer."

Ardy turned from the window, his snout twitching. "And we need to figure out what Ruok's plan is. He's behind all of this."

Lucas clenched his fists. "One step at a time. First, we secure our position here. Then, we gather evidence and plan our next move."

Joanna, her strength slowly returning, spoke up. "There's a scientist on the inside. She's been helping us in secret. She might be able to get us the information we need."

Helen's eyes lit up. "That's our lead. We need to contact her."

As they settled into their temporary safe house, the group discussed their next steps, strategizing late into the night.

Ryan paced the dungeon, his mind racing. They had to get out of there, and fast. Jane and Sebastian were huddled in a corner, whispering urgently.

"We need to come up with a plan," Jane said, her voice steady despite the fear in her eyes. "We can't just sit here and wait for something to happen."

Ryan stopped pacing and faced them. "I've got an idea, but it's risky. We need to lure the guard in here and take him down."

Sebastian frowned. "You mean that ogre? Are you crazy? He's huge!"

Jane nodded thoughtfully. "It's risky, but it's our best shot. We need to create a distraction, make enough noise to get him in here."

Ryan took a deep breath. "Leave that to me."

He began to pound on the cell door, shouting at the top of his lungs. "Hey! Let us out of here! You can't keep us locked up forever!"

The noise echoed through the dungeon, and it wasn't long before they heard the heavy footsteps of the guard approaching. The door creaked open, and the massive ogre stormed in, carrying a boulder.

"That's IT! I've warned you before, and now you'll pay!" the ogre bellowed, his voice reverberating off the stone walls.

As the ogre advanced, Jane and Sebastian grabbed rocks from the floor and hurled them at him. The rocks bounced harmlessly off his thick skin, but it was enough to make him pause.

"Is that all you've got?" the ogre sneered, raising the boulder.

Ryan seized the moment, lunging at the ogre and grabbing onto his arm. "Now, Jane! Sebastian! Help me!"

Jane and Sebastian rushed forward, grabbing at the ogre's legs and trying to knock him off balance. The ogre roared in anger, swinging the boulder wildly. The struggle was intense, but they managed to trip the ogre, sending him crashing to the ground.

"Get the keys!" Ryan shouted, pinning the ogre's arm.

Sebastian scrambled to the ogre's belt, fumbling with the keys. "Got it!"

With the ogre subdued, they quickly unlocked their shackles and made a run for it. The dungeon corridor seemed to stretch on forever, but they kept running, adrenaline fueling their escape.

Bursting out of the dungeon, they found themselves in a vibrant, otherworldly landscape. The streets were filled with people celebrating, music blaring from every corner. It was a dimension of festivals and parties.

"We need to blend in," Jane said, scanning the crowd. "If the guards are looking for us, this is our best chance."

They quickly ducked into the throng of revellers, moving with the flow of the crowd. The colourful costumes and masks provided perfect cover as they navigated through the festivities.

Sebastian glanced around nervously. "Do you think the guards are still after us?"

Ryan nodded. "Definitely. We need to keep moving and find a place to hide."

As they wove through the crowd, they overheard snippets of conversation. It seemed that the guards were working for Ruok and had set up a base in this dimension.

"Ruok must be controlling this place," Jane said, her brow furrowing.

As they moved into the festival; their eyes peeled for any sign of the guards. The celebrations were a dizzying array of colours and sounds, making it both easier and harder to spot danger.

As they passed a booth selling masks, Ryan had an idea. "Let's get some masks. It'll help us blend in even more."

They quickly purchased masks, donning them as they continued through the festival. The masks added an extra layer of anonymity, allowing them to move more freely.

Suddenly, they spotted a group of guards pushing their way through the crowd. Ryan signalled to Jane and Sebastian, and they ducked into an alleyway, holding their breath as the guards passed by.

The portal's swirling colours finally solidified, and Alex, Scarlette, Marcus, stepped into a vibrant city unlike any they had ever seen. The City of Illusions was a kaleidoscope of ever-changing patterns, with buildings that shimmered and morphed, and streets that seemed to shift and twist under their feet.

"Wow, this place is...trippy," Alex remarked, his eyes wide with amazement.

"Stay focused, Alex," Scarlette said, her tone serious. "The riddle stick said the Tick is nearby. We need to find it before the illusions get the best of us."

Marcus nodded, his eyes scanning their surroundings. "Yeah, let's stick together. We don't know what kind of tricks this city might play on us."

As they moved into the city, they noticed that even the walls seemed to be alive, shifting between different colours and textures. It was disorienting, but they kept their focus, driven by the urgency of their mission.

As they turned a corner, they stumbled upon a group of sinister-looking figures. These villains seemed to blend with the city, their forms constantly shifting and changing, making them hard to pin down.

"Look who we have here," one of the villains sneered, his face flickering between a sinister grin and a menacing scowl. "Fresh meat in our city of illusions."

"We're not looking for trouble," Alex said, trying to keep his voice steady. "We just want to find something and leave."

The leader of the villains laughed, a sound that echoed unnervingly off the ever-changing walls. "Oh, but you've already found trouble. Get them!"

The gang was outnumbered and outmatched, but they fought back with everything they had. Scarlette used her ability to manipulate anything red, sending a flurry of crimson objects at their attackers. Marcus, with a quick rap, created a barrier to shield them from harm.

"We can't keep this up!" Scarlette shouted, her eyes darting around for an escape route.

"Over there!" Marcus pointed to a narrow alleyway that seemed to pulse with a softer light. "Run!"

They dashed through the alleyway, bursting into an open plaza filled with floating foods. Super burgers, luminous fruits, and other strange edibles hovered in the air, glowing with an otherworldly light.

"What is this place?" Alex asked, marvelling at the sight.

"No time to wonder," Scarlette said, her eyes on the approaching villains. "Eat something. Maybe it will help."

Without hesitation, Alex grabbed a super burger and took a big bite. Almost instantly, he felt a surge of power course through his veins. He looked at his hands, now glowing with a radiant energy.

"Whoa, I feel incredible!" Alex exclaimed, feeling his strength increase dramatically.

Marcus and Scarlette exchanged glances, then grabbed some floating foods themselves. Marcus started rapping, his words weaving reality around them. "With a rhyme and a beat, I make this power complete!"

Scarlette's eyes turned a vibrant shade of red as she manifested a swirling vortex of red energy. "Time to show these villains what we're made of!"

The villains caught up, but this time, Alex and the gang were ready. Alex soared into the air, his newfound strength allowing him to fly. He unleashed beams of energy from his hands, scattering the villains.

Scarlette, her red powers blazing, created a barrier of crimson light that deflected attacks and sent enemies flying. Marcus rapped furiously, each line bringing objects to life that fought alongside them.

During the battle, Alex spotted the Tick trying to escape. "There it is! Don't let it get away!"

They chased the Tick through the chaotic battlefield, their powers clashing with the illusions and the villains. The Tick was fast and elusive, but Alex's super speed allowed him to keep up. He tackled the Tick, pinning it to the ground.

"We've got you now," Alex said, his grip firm.

The Tick struggled, but Scarlette and Marcus quickly joined him, using their powers to contain it. With a final burst of energy, they destroyed the Tick, which disintegrated into a puff of multicoloured smoke.

From the smoke, a multicoloured ghost coin appeared, hovering in the air. Alex reached out and grabbed it, feeling its strange energy pulse through him.

They all gathered, breathing heavily but triumphant. "We did it," Alex said, holding up the ghost coin. "We did it."

Scarlette smiled, her red eyes returning to normal. "Nice work, everyone."

"How could you keep something like that from us?" Marcus snapped, turning to Scarlette. "You had powers all this time, and you didn't say a word!"

Scarlette's eyes flashed with anger. "Oh, don't act all high and mighty, Marcus. You were keeping your powers a secret too! I was planning on telling everyone, but I needed the right moment."

Marcus crossed his arms, his voice dripping with sarcasm. "Right, because there's always a perfect moment to drop a bombshell like that. You're a real piece of work, Scarlette."

"You're calling me a hypocrite?" Scarlette shot back. "At least I wasn't actively hiding it. I was waiting for the right time.

Alex stepped between them, his frustration evident. "Enough! We don't have time for this bickering. We have more important things to worry about, like finding my son. We need to work together, not tear each other apart."

Marcus and Scarlette glared at each other for a moment longer before storming off in opposite directions. The tension between them was palpable, and Alex felt a knot of frustration tightening in his chest.

"Well, I'm glad you did. Let's get out of here before the city throws any more surprises at us."

They made their way back to the portal, the city of illusions shifting and changing behind them. With the ghost coin in hand, they stepped through, ready for whatever lay ahead.

The portal shimmered and pulsed with light, beckoning Alex, Scarlette, Marcus, and the rest of the gang into yet another dimension. Stepping through, they found themselves in a vibrant city alive with the sounds of music, laughter, and the aroma of mouth-watering foods. The City of Festivals was an endless celebration, with every street filled with people dancing, playing instruments, and indulging in culinary delights.

"Wow, this place is incredible," Alex marvelled, his eyes wide as he took in the colourful sights around them. "It's like one giant party."

"Yeah, it's great," Marcus said, but his tone was anything but enthusiastic. He shot a sideways glance at Scarlette, his jaw clenched.

Scarlette noticed the look and crossed her arms, her expression defiant. "What's your problem, Marcus?"

"My problem?" Marcus echoed, his voice rising. "You're grilling me about keeping my powers secret, but you had your powers this whole time! Talk about hypocrisy."

Scarlette's eyes flashed with anger. "I was going to tell you, unlike you who kept it a secret until it was convenient."

Alex stepped between them, holding up his hands. "Hey, calm down, both of you. This isn't helping."

Marcus scoffed. "Easy for you to say, Alex. You didn't know about her powers either."

"No, I didn't," Alex admitted, looking between them. "But we have more important things to worry about right now, finding my son is more important now."

Scarlette looked away, her expression softening slightly. "Alex is right. We can argue about this later."

Marcus shook his head. "Sure, just like you planned to tell us later, right?"

Scarlette opened her mouth to retort, but Alex cut her off. "Enough! We don't have time for this. According to the riddle stick, my son is nearby. We need to focus on finding him."

There was a tense silence as the festival around them continued in full swing, oblivious to their inner turmoil.

Finally, Marcus muttered, "Fine. But don't think this is over." He turned and stormed off into the crowd, disappearing among the revellers.

Scarlette watched him go; her fists clenched at her sides. "Unbelievable."

"Let him go," Alex said wearily. "We need to stay focused. We'll find him later."

Scarlette nodded reluctantly; her gaze still fixed on the spot where Marcus had vanished. "Let's find your son."

They moved through the bustling streets, the sounds of celebration growing louder as they went. Alex's heart pounded with a mix of anxiety and anticipation. He clutched the riddle stick, hoping it would lead them to his son soon.

As they walked, Scarlette glanced at Alex. "Do you think we got our powers from our previous adventures in other dimensions?"

"It's possible," Alex replied. "Esmeria has a way of changing people. We could have picked up these abilities without even realizing it."

Scarlette sighed. "I guess that makes sense. Still, it's a lot to take in."

"Tell me about it," Alex muttered. "But right now, all that matters is finding my son."

They continued their search, weaving through the throngs of festival-goers. Alex kept his eyes peeled for any sign of his son, hoping against hope that the riddle stick's guidance was accurate.

Meanwhile, Marcus wandered through the city, his anger simmering just beneath the surface. He couldn't believe Scarlette's audacity. She had kept her powers a secret, just like him, and now she was acting like she was in the right.

"Unbelievable," he muttered to himself, kicking at a loose cobblestone. "Just unbelievable."

As he walked, his mind raced with thoughts of their adventures. They had faced so many challenges together, and now this secret was threatening to tear them apart. He couldn't shake the feeling of betrayal, but he also knew they had bigger problems to deal with.

"I need to clear my head," he said, looking around for a quieter spot. The festival was too loud, too chaotic. He needed to think.

He found a small alleyway that seemed to offer some respite from the noise and ducked into it. Leaning against the wall, he closed his eyes and took a deep breath.

"Get it together, Marcus," he told himself. "You can't let this distract you. Alex needs us. We need to find his son."

He took another deep breath, trying to calm his racing thoughts. The festival sounds were muffled here, and he could almost hear himself think.

"Maybe she's right," he admitted quietly

He shook his head, pushing the thoughts away. "Focus. Just focus on the mission."

Back in the main part of the festival, Alex and Scarlette were making their way through the crowded streets. The riddle sticks glowed faintly, pointing them in the right direction.

"We're getting closer," Alex said, his voice filled with determination. "I can feel it."

Scarlette nodded, her own resolve strengthening. "We'll find him, Alex. I promise."

They continued on, the festival's energy buzzing around them. As they rounded a corner, the riddle stick pulsed brightly, indicating that they were near their goal.

"There!" Alex pointed to a small, secluded area where a few people were gathered, seemingly enjoying a quieter part of the festival.

They approached cautiously, their eyes scanning the area for any sign of Alex's son.

Marcus and Scarlette had separated after their argument, each lost in their thoughts and emotions. The City of Festivals, with its unending celebration, provided a temporary distraction from the tension that had built up between them.

Marcus wandered through the lively streets, the vibrant colours and sounds a stark contrast to his turbulent emotions. He found himself at the heart of the festivities, where a large stage had been set up. People from various dimensions had gathered, their unique appearances and stories creating a kaleidoscope of cultures and experiences.

"Welcome, welcome!" a voice boomed from the stage. Marcus looked up to see a charismatic host with a wide grin. "Today, we celebrate the convergence of dimensions! Share your stories, and your talents, and let's make this a night to remember!"

The crowd cheered, and Marcus couldn't help but feel a spark of excitement. He had always loved performing, and this seemed like the perfect opportunity to clear his head and maybe even impress the locals.

He stepped forward, making his way through the crowd to the stage. As he approached, the host noticed him and waved him up. "Come on up, friend! What's your name and where are you from?"

Marcus took the microphone, his confidence returning. "Name's Marcus and I'm from... well, let's just say a place far from here."

The host chuckled. "Aren't we all? What talent do you bring to our festival today, Marcus?"

Marcus grinned, feeling the familiar thrill of performing. "I rap. And I can make things happen with my rhymes."

The host's eyebrows shot up in surprise. "Now that's something we've got to see! Ladies and gentlemen, give it up for Marcus!"

The crowd erupted in applause as Marcus took centre stage. A beat started playing, and he felt the rhythm flow through him. He began to rap, his words weaving a tapestry of imagery and power.

"From the streets to the skies, where the festival lies,

I'm Marcus, the magician, with a lyrical surprise.

Watch the magic unfold as I spit these rhymes,

Manifesting wonders, transcending all times."

As he rapped, objects began to materialize around him. A shower of colourful confetti rained down, and sparkling lights danced in the air. The crowd gasped in amazement, their faces lit with delight.

Marcus continued, feeling the energy of the crowd feed his performance.

"Floating in the rhythm, like a dream come true,

Turning thoughts into things, right in front of you.

From fire to flowers, from gold to gleam,

This is the magic of Marcus, living the dream."

He summoned fireworks that exploded in brilliant colours above the stage, drawing cheers and applause from the audience. It felt good to be in his element, to share his talent and see the joy it brought to others.

Meanwhile, Scarlette had found herself in a quieter part of the city. She sat at a small outdoor café, sipping a drink and watching the festival goers pass by. Her thoughts were a whirlwind of emotions, but she was determined to make the most of the evening.

"Mind if I join you?" a voice asked, interrupting her thoughts.

She looked up to see a woman with striking blue hair and an ethereal presence. "Sure," Scarlette replied, gesturing to the empty seat.

" the woman introduced herself, sitting down. "From the Dimension of Echoes. And you are?"

"Scarlette," she replied. "From... well, let's just say a different dimension."

The woman smiled. "Seems like we're all from different places today. That's the beauty of this festival, isn't it? So many stories, so many worlds converging in one place."

Scarlette nodded, feeling a bit more at ease. "Yeah, it's pretty amazing. What brings you here?"

The woman's eyes sparkled with excitement. "I'm a storyteller. I travel between dimensions, collecting tales and sharing them wherever I go. And you?"

Scarlette hesitated, unsure of how much to reveal. "I'm... on a mission, I guess. With some friends. But now, I'm just trying to enjoy the festival."

The woman nodded understandingly. "We all need a break sometimes. If you don't mind, I'd love to hear your story."

Scarlette found herself opening up, sharing bits and pieces of their adventures. As she spoke, she felt a sense of relief, as if a weight was lifting off her shoulders.

Meanwhile, back at the stage, Marcus had finished his performance to thunderous applause. He stepped down, feeling a rush of satisfaction. As he mingled with the crowd, he met various interesting characters, each with their own unique stories.

One was a tall, slender man with glowing tattoos that shifted and changed with his mood. "I'm from the Realm of Light," he explained. "We communicate through these tattoos. They express our emotions and thoughts."

Another was a young woman with wings that shimmered like dragonfly wings. "I'm from the Forest of Whispers," she said. "Our wings allow us to hear the voices of nature and communicate with the trees and animals."

Marcus listened, fascinated by the diversity of the festival goers. He shared his own story, the challenges they had faced, and the powers they had discovered.

A sudden hush fell over the crowd. The music stopped, and an eerie silence settled over the festival. Marcus looked around, confused, as a group of figures emerged from the shadows.

The Hell Defenders had arrived.

They were a formidable sight, clad in dark, intimidating armour that seemed to absorb the light around them. Eltscar, Scarlette's evil double doppelgänger, her eyes cold and calculating.

"Enjoying the party?" Eltscar's voice dripped with sarcasm. "Sorry to cut it short."

The crowd parted in fear as Eltscar raised her plasma pack weapon. Before anyone could react, she fired a stream of power-draining slime directly at Scarlette, who had just arrived at the scene.

Scarlette screamed as the slime hit her, sapping her strength and rendering her powerless. She fell to her knees, her eyes wide with fear and pain.

"Help me, Marcus!" she cried out, her voice desperate.

Marcus's heart pounded in his chest as he watched in horror. He started to run towards her, but the Hell Defenders were too quick. They grabbed Scarlette, dragging her towards a portal they had summoned.

"Let her go!" Marcus shouted, but his voice was lost in the chaos. The crowd was panicking, people were fleeing in all directions, and the festival had turned into a scene of terror.

Eltscar sneered at Marcus, her grip on Scarlette unrelenting. "Too late, hero. She's coming with us."

With that, she and the Hell Defenders stepped through the portal, taking Scarlette with them. The portal closed with a flash, leaving Marcus standing there, helpless and enraged.

He clenched his fists, his mind racing. He needed to save Scarlette, but he couldn't do it alone.

"Scarlette!" Marcus screamed, his voice barely audible over the chaos around him. The festival crowd, now a frenzy of fear and confusion, surged in all directions, making it difficult for Marcus to push through.

He witnessed Scarlette's desperate struggle as the Hell Defenders dragged her toward the portal. Every fibre of his being screamed to reach her, to save her, but the crowd seemed an insurmountable barrier. His heart pounded in his chest, a mix of fear and rage driving him forward.

"Move! Get out of the way!" Marcus shouted, shoving his way through the throng of panicked festival-goers. The portal, shimmering with a dark, ominous energy, was slowly closing, the gap between its edges narrowing with each passing second.

Scarlette's terrified eyes met his for a brief moment, a silent plea for help that tore at his soul. "I'm coming, Scarlette!" Marcus yelled, his voice cracking with desperation. He could see Eltscar's cruel smirk as she tightened her grip on Scarlette, pulling her closer to the portal's edge.

Just as the portal's closing speed began to accelerate, Marcus reached the clearing. With a final, desperate lunge, he threw himself forward, his body hurtling toward the shrinking gateway. The edges of the portal shimmered and crackled with energy, threatening to seal shut.

In an adrenaline-fueled leap, Marcus dove headfirst into the portal, feeling the strange, cold sensation of its energy wash over him. He tumbled through the other side, landing hard on the ground as the portal sealed itself with a resounding snap behind him. He was in an unfamiliar, dark dimension, but he had made it. Now, he just had to find Scarlette.

Amidst the chaos of the festival, Alex was single-mindedly focused on his goal: finding his son, Ryan. The riddle stick pulsed brightly in his hand, guiding him through the maze of terrified festival-goers. He could feel his heart pounding in his chest, a mix of anxiety driving him forward.

"Ryan! Where are you?" Alex called out, his voice strained with worry. He scanned the crowd, his eyes darting from face to face, hoping to catch a glimpse of his son. The festival's vibrant energy had turned into a frantic scramble, and it seemed like everyone was moving in the opposite direction.

Then, in a brief moment of clarity, he saw them. Ryan, Jane, and Sebastian stood together in the crowd, their faces a mix of fear and confusion. Relief washed over Alex as he ran towards them, his heart lifting at the sight of his son.

"Ryan!" Alex shouted, his voice breaking with emotion. He reached them and pulled his son into a tight hug, holding him close as if he might disappear. "Thank goodness you're safe."

"Dad!" Ryan exclaimed, hugging him back just as tightly. "We were so worried about you!"

Alex pulled back slightly, looking into his son's eyes. "I'm sorry, Ryan. I'm sorry for everything. For being insensitive, for not understanding your perspective. I was so caught up in my own past that I forgot to see things from your point of view."

Ryan shook his head, a small smile forming on his lips. "It's okay, Dad. I know you just want to protect me. I need to understand that your experiences shape how you see things. We'll figure it out together."

Jane and Sebastian nodded in agreement, their expressions softening. Jane spoke up, her voice gentle. "We know you're trying your best, Alex. And we appreciate it."

Ryan took a deep breath, his face growing serious. "Dad, we saw something. Those evil doppelgängers, they kidnapped Scarlette. And Marcus... he jumped into the portal after them. The portal's still there, slowly closing."

Alex's heart sank. "What? Where? Show me!"

CHAPTER NINE

THE FESTIVAL ATTACK

Ryan pointed towards the edge of the festival, where the portal's glow was still visible. Without another word, Alex grabbed Ryan's hand and started running, with Jane and Sebastian following closely behind.

As the dust settled from the initial chaos of the festival attack, Alex, Ryan, Sebastian, and Jane stood together, catching their breath and gathering their thoughts. The festival had been transformed from a place of celebration to a battlefield in a matter of moments, and they were all acutely aware of the danger that still loomed.

Suddenly, Ryan's eyes widened with alarm as he spotted a new threat emerging from the shadows. "Dad, look! It's Ruok's guards. We have to move, now!" His voice was urgent, and Alex followed his son's gaze to see the massive, intimidating figures of Ruok's ogre guards pushing through the panicked crowd.

"Everyone, follow me!" Ryan shouted, taking charge of the situation. "We need to get to the portal before it's too late!"

They didn't have a moment to lose. The guards were closing in, their towering forms and menacing expressions striking fear into the hearts of those around them. Alex, Ryan, Sebastian, and Jane began to weave through the throng of festival-goers, trying to stay out of sight and avoid confrontation.

"Stay low and keep moving," Alex instructed, his voice tense but steady. "We can't afford to get caught now."

Jane nodded, her face pale but resolute. "We can do this. Just stick together."

Sebastian, always quick on his feet, took point alongside Ryan. "This way!" he called out, leading them through a narrow alley that offered a temporary reprieve from the chaos.

As they moved, Alex kept glancing over his shoulder, ensuring they weren't being followed too closely. The ogre guards were relentless, their heavy footsteps and gruff voices echoing ominously behind them. "Faster," Alex urged. "The portal won't stay open forever."

They emerged from the alley into a more open area, where the festival's remnants were still scattered. The portal's was visible in the distance, flickering and shrinking with each passing second. It was now or never.

"There it is!" Ryan pointed, his voice filled with both hope and desperation. "We have to reach it before it closes!"

The group broke into a full sprint, their legs pumping with adrenaline and fear. The portal loomed ahead, its shimmering edges tantalizingly close yet maddeningly out of reach. The crowd seemed to part before them, as if sensing their urgency and stepping aside just in time.

But the ogre guards were gaining. Their sheer size and brute strength allowed them to bulldoze through obstacles, and they were closing the distance rapidly. "Don't look back!" Ryan shouted, his focus unwavering. "Just keep running!"

As they neared the portal, the energy around it became more intense, crackling with power. The edges of the portal were nearly touching, but there was still a small gap—just enough for them to make it through.

Ryan reached the portal first, his determination driving him forward. He glanced back to ensure the others were right behind him. "Go, go, go!" he urged, his voice filled with urgency.

One by one, they dove through the portal, the cold, disorienting sensation enveloping them as they crossed the threshold. Alex was the last to jump, his heart pounding as he felt the portal begin to close around him. With a final, desperate leap, he propelled himself through, landing hard on the other side just as the portal sealed shut with a resounding snap.

Emerging from the portal, Alex, Ryan, Sebastian, and Jane found themselves in a strange dimension. The air shimmered with an otherworldly glow, and the landscape was dotted with structures and contraptions, each one a puzzle or game waiting to be solved. The ground beneath their feet felt unstable, shifting slightly with each step.

"This place is... unsettling," Jane said, her voice hushed with awe.

Ryan nodded, his eyes scanning their surroundings. "Stay alert. We don't know what kinds of traps or challenges are waiting for us."

In the distance, they spotted Marcus, who was pacing anxiously near a massive, intricate structure. His face was etched with worry, He looked up as they approached, relief washing over his features.

"Alex, you made it," Marcus said, his voice tinged with a mixture of relief and urgency. "Scarlette is trapped in some kind of contraption. We have to save her," Marcus said, his voice trembling with urgency.

"We'll do whatever it takes," Alex replied firmly. "Tell us what we need to do."

Marcus gestured to the various puzzles and games scattered around them. "These puzzles seem to be the key. We have to solve them to deactivate the traps and free Scarlette. But we need to be careful – failure has deadly consequences."

"Let's not waste any time," Ryan said, stepping forward. "We'll use the riddle stick to help us."

They approached the first puzzle, a towering structure with intricate gears and levers, its metallic parts gleaming ominously. The riddle stick pulsed with a soft glow, guiding them as they began to work together. Each movement was precise, each action deliberate, as they manipulated the gears and levers, solving the complex mechanisms.

"Look at the engravings," Alex pointed out, his brow furrowed in concentration. "They seem to tell a story. Maybe we need to follow it."

"Good catch," Marcus replied, tracing the engravings with his fingers. "It looks like a sequence. Let's align the gears to match it."

As they turned the gears, a low rumble echoed through the chamber, and the puzzle shifted, revealing hidden compartments and mechanisms. They worked methodically, aligning each gear until the structure clicked into place.

"First puzzle down," Ryan said, wiping sweat from his brow. "But that was just the beginning."

A section of the ground shifted, revealing a path to the next challenge. They moved quickly, their hearts pounding with a mixture of fear and determination. The second puzzle was even more daunting, a series of interconnected mazes that required them to navigate carefully to avoid deadly traps.

"Watch your step," Alex cautioned, his eyes focused on the riddle stick. "One wrong move and it's over."

The maze was filled with pressure plates, some of which triggered deadly spikes from the floor and walls. The riddle stick glowed faintly, indicating the safest path, but it was up to them to interpret its guidance accurately.

"Step only where it pulses the brightest," Ryan advised. "And be ready to move fast."

They proceeded cautiously, communicating in whispers to avoid startling one another into a misstep. Each step was nerve-wracking, but their trust in one another grew with each successful move. Halfway through, Alex stumbled and triggered a plate.

"Get down!" Marcus shouted, pulling Alex back as spikes shot up from the ground, narrowly missing them.

"Thanks," Alex panted, regaining his balance. "Let's keep going."

Finally, they reached the end of the maze, their bodies tense with the adrenaline of narrowly escaping death. The third puzzle involved a series of riddles, each one more challenging than the last. The riddle stick glowed brighter with each correct answer, guiding them forward.

"Here's the first one," Marcus read aloud. "'I speak without a mouth and hear without ears. I have no body, but I come alive with wind. What am I?'"

"An echo," Alex answered confidently. The riddle stick brightened, confirming the answer.

"Next one," Ryan said. "'I'm light as a feather, yet the strongest man can't hold me for more than five minutes. What am I?'"

"Breath," Alex said after a moment of thought. The stick glowed again.

As they solved each riddle, the path ahead became clearer, though the puzzles grew increasingly complex. The final riddle stumped them for several minutes until Scarlette's faint voice echoed through the chamber, providing a clue.

Finally, they reached the last puzzle, a massive contraption that held Scarlette captive. She was suspended in a complex web of wires and machinery, her face pale but resolute.

"Scarlette!" Marcus called out, his voice filled with desperation. "We're here. We're going to get you out."

Scarlette managed a weak smile. "Be careful. The Hell Defenders are nearby."

Alex and the others approached the contraption, their minds focused on the task at hand. The riddle stick guided them as they worked to deactivate the traps and free Scarlette. The machinery was a tangle of gears, levers, and wires, all interconnected in a mind-boggling array.

"Let's divide the tasks," Alex suggested. "Marcus, you handle the gears. Ryan, take the levers. I'll focus on the wires."

Each movement was precise, and each action deliberated, as they navigated the complex machinery. Marcus carefully adjusted the gears, his hands steady despite the urgency. Ryan manipulated the levers with calculated precision, listening for the telltale clicks that signalled progress. Alex traced the wires, his eyes darting between the riddle stick and the contraption.

"Almost there," Ryan muttered, his fingers trembling as he pulled a lever into place.

"Got it," Marcus said, locking the final gear into position.

Finally, with a final, decisive action, the contraption released its hold on Scarlette, and she fell into Marcus's waiting arms. They embraced tightly, relief flooding over them.

"We did it," Marcus whispered, his voice choked with emotion. "We saved you."

Scarlette nodded, her eyes filled with gratitude. "Thank you. All of you."

Suddenly, a shimmering light appeared above them, and a set of weapons materialized out of thin air. Alex and his friends stared in awe as they realized what they were seeing.

"The Air Blasters," Ryan said, his voice filled with wonder. "They're incredible."

Alex picked up one of the weapons, feeling its weight and power. "I've missed this," he said, a smile spreading across his face. "Let's see what these can do."

They turned to see the Hell Defenders standing nearby, their backs turned to them. Without hesitation, Alex aimed his Air Blaster and shouted, "Hey! Ugly usses!"

The Hell Defenders whirled around, their faces contorted with surprise. Alex and his friends fired their Air Blasters, sending powerful blasts of air that hit the Hell Defenders with incredible force. The enemies were lifted off their feet and sent flying through the air, disappearing into a swirling portal.

"That was amazing," Sebastian said, a grin spreading across his face. "These Air Blasters are incredible."

"Yeah, they are," Jane agreed, her eyes shining with excitement. "We did it."

Marcus and Scarlette turned to each other, their faces filled with a mixture of relief and guilt. "I'm sorry," Marcus said, his voice earnest. "I shouldn't have let our argument get in the way."

Scarlette shook her head, her eyes softening. "I'm sorry too. We need to be united, especially now."

They leaned in and shared a tender kiss, their bond stronger than ever. As they pulled away, Alex approached, a look of determination on his face.

"We need to get out of here," Alex said. "The portal is closing."

They turned to see the portal, its edges shrinking with each passing moment. Without hesitation, they sprinted towards it, their hearts pounding with urgency. One by one, they leapt through the portal, feeling the disorienting sensation of crossing dimensions.

They landed in a dark, foreboding place, the air heavy with an oppressive energy. The ground was uneven, and shadows seemed to move of their own accord.

Alex, Ryan, Sebastian, Jane, Marcus, and Scarlette stumbled through the dark, swirling portal, emerging into a nightmarish realm. The air was thick with an oppressive darkness, and the ground beneath their feet felt uneven and unstable. Twisted trees loomed overhead, their branches like skeletal fingers reaching for the sky. Shadows shifted and twisted, giving the eerie illusion that they were being watched from every direction.

"This place... it's like a twisted version of the world we know," Jane said, her voice barely a whisper.

Ryan nodded, his eyes scanning their surroundings. "Stay close. We don't know what's lurking in the shadows."

As they move closely into the dark dimension, grotesque monsters and the stuff of nightmares begin to emerge from the shadows. Hideous creatures with elongated limbs, snarling fangs, and glowing red eyes stalked them, their growls and hisses sending shivers down their spines. The team moved cautiously, their senses on high alert.

"Just keep moving," Alex urged, gripping his Air Blaster tightly. "We have to find a way out of here."

They pressed on, their footsteps echoing silence. Suddenly, a massive figure emerged from the darkness, towering over them. It was Ruok, still in his werewolf-like form but now clad in dark, menacing armour and a flowing cloak. His eyes glowed with a malevolent light, and he seemed even more formidable than before.

"Welcome to my world, Alex," Ruok boomed, his voice echoing through the twisted landscape. "You may have destroyed the Ticks that gave me power, foiled my plans of invincibility, and saved your son, but that doesn't mean I haven't gained enough power to take over your world, thanks to my Hell Defenders draining your friend's powers."

The Hell Defenders, standing by Ruok's side, smirked smugly at his praise. Their dark, intimidating presence added to the palpable sense of danger.

"You don't have your Ghost coins to save you this time, do you, old boy?" Ruok taunted, his voice dripping with contempt.

Alex squared his shoulders, meeting Ruok's gaze with steely determination. "We don't need Ghost coins to defeat you, Ruok. We've faced worse than you, and we'll do it again."

Ryan stepped forward, his voice filled with resolve. "You think you can scare us with your twisted world and your Hell Defenders? We're not backing down."

Ruok let out a low, menacing chuckle. "Brave words for a boy who has no idea of the true power I possess. This realm bends to my will. You are nothing but insects to be crushed under my heel."

Scarlette tightened her grip on Marcus's hand, her eyes blazing with anger. "We won't let you take over our world, Ruok. We've already defeated you once, and we can do it again."

The Hell Defenders advanced, their weapons at the ready. Eltscar, Scarlette's evil double, sneered at them. "You think you can stop us? You're just delaying the inevitable."

Alex glanced at his team, a silent understanding passing between them. They had come too far, faced too many dangers, to let Ruok win now.

Alex's grip tightened on his Air Blaster. Like I said earlier "We don't need Ghost coins to defeat you, Ruok. We've faced worse than you, and we'll do it again."

Ruok sneered. "Brave words for a man standing on the precipice of his doom."

Suddenly, Scarlette's eyes widened as she spotted a faint glow in the distance, a portal shimmering with a promise of escape. "Alex, look!" she shouted, pointing. "A portal! We need to go through it. Ruok is too powerful to defeat in his world."

Alex's face contorted with rage. "He kidnapped my son! I'm not running away from him!"

Ryan stepped forward, placing a hand on his father's shoulder. "Dad, sometimes retreating is the smartest move. We can come back stronger."

Scarlette nodded. "We need to survive to fight another day, Alex. If we stay, we risk everything."

Alex's anger was palpable, but he knew they were right. "Alright," he said reluctantly. "Let's go."

With that, Alex, Marcus, Scarlette, Ryan, Sebastian, and Jane made a break for the portal. Ruok roared in fury, realizing their plan. "Stop them!" he commanded, and the Hell Defenders surged forward, weapons raised.

The group ran as fast as they could, dodging the attacks from the Hell Defenders. Alex fired his Air Blaster, sending blasts of air to clear a path. Marcus rapped spells that created barriers, blocking the

Defenders' attacks. Scarlette used her power to manipulate objects, creating obstacles to slow down their pursuers.

"We're almost there!" Jane shouted, her voice filled with hope.

Just as they reached the portal, Ruok lunged forward, his massive form looming over them. "You can't escape me!" he bellowed, his claws slashing through the air.

Alex turned, his face, "Get through the portal! I'll hold him off!"

"No, Dad!" Ryan shouted. "We go together!"

Marcus nodded. "We fight as one. No one gets left behind."

Scarlette's eyes blazed with resolve. "We're stronger together, Alex. Trust us."

Alex hesitated but then nodded. "Alright. On three, we all jump. One… two… three!"

They leapt into the portal just as Ruok's claws came down.

After they emerged from the portal, disoriented but were relieved to find themselves back in the familiar streets of London outside Alex's mum's house.

Alex, Marcus, Scarlette, Ryan, Sebastian, and Jane gathered their bearings, feeling the weight of their recent battles heavy on their shoulders.

"We need to lay low for a while," Alex said, looking around warily. "Ruok and his Hell Defenders might still be after us."

Marcus nodded in agreement. "Yeah, we need to regroup and figure out our next move."

Scarlette glanced at Alex, concern etched on her face. "Where can we go that's safe?"

Alex's expression softened. "My mum's house. She's been ill, but it's the safest place I can think of right now."

Sebastian scoffed, crossing his arms. "Great, just what we need. Hiding out in some old lady's house. This is a brilliant plan."

Ryan frowned at Sebastian. "Do you have a better idea?"

Sebastian rolled his eyes. "No, but it doesn't mean I have to like this one either.

Jane stepped in, trying to calm the tension. "Look, we're all tired and stressed. Let's just get somewhere "

As they moved through the crowded streets until they reached a quaint, modest house. The door opened before they could knock, and Helen, Mr. Ransford, Lucas, and Ardy greeted them with worried expressions.

"Alex!" Helen exclaimed, rushing to embrace him. "We've been so worried!"

Mr. Ransford stepped forward; his face lined with concern. "We've been looking after your mother. She's... she's not doing well, Alex."

Alex's heart sank. "I need to see her."

They led Alex and the group inside, where they found Joanna Knight, Alex's mum lying in bed, looking frail and weakened. The mutation had taken a heavy toll on her, and it was evident that she was struggling.

"Mum," Alex whispered, kneeling by her side. "I'm so sorry. I couldn't destroy Ruok."

Joanna's eyes opened, and a weak smile spread across her lips. "Alex... my dear boy. You saved your son. That's what matters."

Ryan, tears streaming down his face, rushed to his grandmother's side and hugged her tightly. "Grandma, I'm so sorry. I love you so much."

Joanna gently stroked Ryan's hair, her voice soothing despite her condition. "I love you too, Ryan. You're all so brave. Don't ever forget that."

Scarlette, Marcus, Sebastian, Jane, and the others gathered around, their expressions sombre as they watched the touching family moment. Joanna's strength and kindness shone through, even in her weakened state.

"I'm so proud of all of you," Joanna said softly, her gaze sweeping over the group. "You've faced unimaginable challenges and come out stronger. Never lose hope."

Alex's eyes filled with tears as he held his mother's hand. "I wish I could have done more, Mum. I wish I could have saved you."

Joanna shook her head weakly. "You've done more than enough, Alex. Your love and courage have given me so much joy. Remember that."

Ryan clung to his grandmother, his sobs echoing through the room. "Don't go, Grandma. Please don't go."

Joanna's breath grew shallow, but she managed a gentle smile. "It's time for me to rest, Ryan. But I'll always be with you. In your heart."

With those final words, Joanna Knight's eyes closed, and she took her last breath. The room was filled with a heavy silence as everyone grappled with the loss.

Helen wrapped her arms around her husband, Alex, both of them overcome with grief. "She was an incredible woman, Alex," Helen whispered, her voice choked with emotion. "We'll get through this together."

Marcus placed a comforting hand on Ryan's shoulder. "Your grandmother was right, Ryan. We've got each other. We'll face whatever comes next, just like she wanted us to."

Scarlette wiped away her tears, "We owe it to her to keep fighting. To protect our world and make her proud."

Mr. Ransford nodded, his voice steady despite his sorrow. "Joanna was a strong woman, Let's honour her memory by staying strong."

As if things couldn't get any worse, London began to change in horrifying ways that mirrored the dark dimensions they had just escaped. It started subtly—a chill in the air, a strange sense of foreboding. But sooner, the city transformed into a nightmarish version of itself, as if the very fabric of reality was being twisted by a malevolent force.

The River Thames, once a tourist-view arena of the city's vibrancy, turned into a river of blood. The crimson water flowed sluggishly, its surface rippling with an unnatural sheen. The smell of iron and decay filled the air, causing passersby to cover their noses in horror and confusion.

Minotaurs creatures roamed the desolate landscape, their eyes glowing with an unholy light as they searched for prey. Other hellish beasts prowled the area, their growls and roars creating a terror that reverberated through the city streets.

The public's reaction to the horror was immediate and visceral. Screams of panic filled the air as people fled in all directions, desperate to escape the nightmarish scenes unfolding around them. Parents clutched their children tightly, trying to shield them from the horrors. Strangers huddled together, seeking comfort and safety in numbers.

"What is happening?" a woman cried out, her eyes wide with terror as she stared at the blood-red Thames. "This can't be real!"

A man next to her shook his head, his face pale and drawn. "It's like we've been plunged into hell itself."

At Alex's mum's house, the group watched in stunned silence as the city outside changed before their eyes. The transformation was swift and brutal, leaving no corner of London untouched.

"This is Ruok's doing," Marcus said grimly, his fists clenched in anger. "He's bringing his world into ours."

"We need to stop this," Scarlette added, her voice trembling with both fear and determination. "But how? We're not ready to face him again."

Ryan looked up at his father, tears still in his eyes but now, "Dad, we have to do something. We can't let this happen."

Alex nodded, his grief over his mother's death mingling with a fierce determination to protect his city and his loved ones. "We'll find a way. We have to."

Helen placed a comforting hand on her husband's shoulder. "We're with you, Alex. Whatever it takes, we'll fight this together." Hugging her son Ryan.

Lucas and Ardy, standing nearby, shared a look of steely resolve. "We're not backing down," Lucas said firmly. "We've come too far to give up now."

Mr. Ransford, ever the voice of wisdom and guidance, stepped forward. "We need a plan. And we need to find allies. There must be others out there who are willing to stand against this darkness."

Just then, a roar echoed from the direction of St James's Park, followed by the sight of a massive Minotaur charging down the street, scattering people in its path. The creature's eyes burned with malevolence as it rampaged through the city, leaving destruction in its wake.

An elderly woman, her hands trembling, clutching a rosary as a spectre floated towards her, its hollow eyes staring into her soul. "Stay back!" she cried, her voice breaking with fear. The ghost paused, its form shimmering before it let out a mournful wail and dissipated into the air.

A young man, his face pale with terror, ran through the streets as demonic figures chased him. "Help! Someone, please help me!" he screamed, glancing over his shoulder at the nightmarish creatures closing in on him. He stumbled and fell, but before the demons could reach him, a group of civilians armed with makeshift weapons intervened, beating back the monsters with sticks and metal pipes.

Families huddled together in their homes, the walls shaking as unseen forces pounded against them. Children cried, clinging to their parents, while their parents tried to comfort them despite their fear. "It's going to be okay," a mother whispered to her son, "We'll get through this."

During this chaos, a portal opened in the heart of the city, and Ruok emerged, flanked by his Hell Defenders. The monstrous figures radiated an aura of darkness and malevolence, their eyes gleaming with sinister intent. Ruok's presence was like a shadow that blotted out the light, and the air around him seemed to grow colder.

"We have come to claim this world," Ruok declared, his voice echoing through the streets. "Submit to the darkness or be consumed by it."

The citizens of London, are already pushed to the brink by the horrors around them. They had been in lockdown, oppressed and terrified by the IDF, who had kidnapped mutant-affected people for experiments. But now, with the truth revealed that Alex and his friends were framed by their evil doppelgängers, the people knew who their true enemies were.

A man in his thirties, wearing a tattered jacket, stood on a makeshift platform and shouted to the gathered crowd. "We've been lied to! Alex and his friends are innocent! It's the IDF and these monsters we should be fighting against!" His words resonated with the crowd, who began to rally around him.

An elderly man, his voice shaking with emotion, raised his cane in defiance. "We won't let these creatures take our city! Fight back, everyone! Use whatever you can find!"

The citizens armed themselves with anything they could get their hands on—bats, kitchen knives, even pieces of debris from the ruined buildings. They formed makeshift barricades and stood ready to defend their city.

At Alex's mum's house, the group watched the growing revolt with a mix of hope and apprehension. "The people are fighting back," Marcus said, a note of awe in his voice. "They're not just running anymore."

Ryan looked up at his father, determination shining in his young eyes. "We have to help them, Dad. We can't let them fight alone."

Alex placed a hand on his son's shoulder, his expression resolute. "You're right, Ryan. We're going to join them. Together, we'll take back our city."

Helen hugged her son tightly before turning to the group. "Be careful out there. We'll be with you in spirit."

Mr Ransford, ever the voice of wisdom, spoke up. "Remember, this is about more than just fighting the monsters. It's about showing everyone that we won't be controlled by fear. That we can stand up against darkness."

As the group prepared to head out, the sound of the riot grew louder. Citizens clashed with both the IDF and the monstrous invaders, their courage and determination evident in every swing of a bat or thrust of a makeshift spear.

A woman in her twenties, her hair dishevelled and eyes blazing with defiance, swung a chair leg at an approaching demon. "For our city!" she shouted, the force of her blow sending the creature reeling.

Nearby, an older man wielding a broom fought off an IDF soldier, his face set in grim determination. "You won't take any more of us!" he roared, knocking the soldier to the ground.

In the chaos, the news spread like wildfire. Central London had become a battleground, with citizens rising against their oppressors. The footage showed ordinary people fighting side by side with Alex and his friends, their combined efforts driving back the darkness.

As the group approached a particularly fierce battle, Alex raised his air blaster and shouted to the people around him. "Stay strong! We're all in this together!"

Marcus, standing beside him, added, "Don't give up! We've faced worse and come out stronger!"

Encouraged by the sight of ordinary citizens fighting back against the nightmarish invaders, Alex, Scarlette, Mr. Ransford, Lucas, and Ardy decided it was time to come out of hiding. They couldn't stand by while people were getting hurt. The group gathered in the living room, the weight of their decision heavy but necessary.

"We can't stay here any longer," Alex said, his voice resolute. "The people need us. We have to help them fight."

Helen's eyes filled with worry, but she nodded. "I understand, Alex. I'll stay here with your mother and the kids. You go and do what you have to do."

Alex leaned in and kissed her gently. "Thank you, Helen. Take care of them for me."

Helen smiled through her tears. "I will. Be safe out there. We need you."

Ryan hugged his father tightly. "You've done this before, Dad. Go get 'em!"

Alex smiled down at his son, ruffling his hair. "I'll be back, buddy. Keep an eye on your mum and grandma for me."

Lucas, Helen, Ryan, Jane, Sebastien and Ardy stay home with Alex's mum after she passes.

CHAPTER TEN

THE MERCILESS END OF RUOK'S MISSION

Mr. Ransford, his face lined forward. "Let's get those E-Jet packs ready. We've got work to do."

The group suited up with the E-Jet packs from their earlier adventures, the familiar hum of the engines a comforting reminder of past victories. They knew this would be a challenging fight, but they were ready.

As they soared into the sky, the city of London spread out below them like a hellish landscape. The air was thick with smoke and the cries of the frightened and the dying. Winged beasts, their eyes glowing with malevolence, swooped down upon the city, adding to the chaos.

"Stay close and keep your eyes open!" Alex shouted over the roar of the engines. "We've got to make it to Central London in one piece."

Scarlette, her eyes scanning the skies, called out, "Incoming! From the left!"

A massive, winged demon hurtled towards them; its claws extended. Alex and the others swerved to avoid its attack, but the beast was relentless.

"Watch out!" Marcus yelled, firing his air blaster at the creature. The blast hit the demon square in the chest, but it barely slowed down.

"These things are tougher than they look!" Mr Ransford shouted, dodging another attack. "Keep firing! Don't let them get close!"

The group engaged in a fierce aerial battle, their E-Jet packs allowing them to manoeuvre quickly, but the winged beasts were fast and aggressive. Scarlette blasted one demon with a concentrated burst of energy, sending it spiralling down into the streets below.

"Nice shot, Scarlette!" Alex called out, firing at another creature. "We've got to keep moving!"

They flew through the chaos, dodging attacks and firing back with their air blasters. The intensity of the battle was overwhelming, but they pressed on, determined to reach Central London and join the fight.

Finally, they landed, where the battle between the public and the monsters was raging. The sight was both horrifying and inspiring. Ordinary citizens, armed with makeshift weapons, were holding their ground against the hellish invaders.

"We're here to help!" Alex shouted, raising his air blaster. "Let's take these monsters down!"

Marcus and Scarlette joined Alex as they confronted Ruok and the Hell Defenders. The air crackled with tension as the two sides faced off.

Ruok sneered, his eyes glowing with dark energy. "So, you've come to die with your precious humans. How noble."

Alex stepped forward, his grip tight on his air blaster. "We're here to stop you, Ruok. This ends now."

Ruok laughed, a sound that sent chills down the spines of everyone present. "You think you can stop me? You're nothing compared to the power I wield."

With a roar, Ruok unleashed a wave of dark energy, but Alex, Marcus, and Scarlette were ready. They fired their air blasters in unison, the blasts colliding with Ruok's attack and creating a shockwave that shook the ground.

The Hell Defenders charged forward, their monstrous forms bristling with dark power. Marcus and Scarlette took aim and fired, their blasts tearing through the ranks of the Hell Defenders but the creatures fought back fiercely.

"Stay focused!" Alex shouted, dodging an attack from a Hell Defender. "We can't let them overwhelm us!"

Marcus fired a blast at a Hell Defender, sending it reeling. "These things are tough, but we can take them down!"

Scarlette, added, "For Joanna! For our city!" She fired at another Hell Defender, her shot hitting it squarely in the chest.

Ruok watched the battle with a sinister smile. "You can't win. My Hell Defenders are unstoppable."

Alex turned his attention back to Ruok. "We'll see about that." He fired his air blaster, the blast narrowly missing Ruok as the dark lord dodged.

The battle was fierce and unrelenting. The Hell Defenders put up a formidable fight, their dark powers making them formidable opponents.

A young woman, her face smeared with dirt and blood, swung a broken chair leg at a demon, her eyes filled with fierce, "We won't let you take our city!"

An older man, his voice hoarse from shouting, rallied a group of civilians. "Stand together! We can do this!"

The battle raged on, the sounds of conflict filling the air. Alex and his friends fought with everything they had, their determination unwavering despite the odds.

Ruok, his frustration growing, unleashed another wave of dark energy. "You can't win! This world will be mine!"

Alex gritted his teeth, his resolve steeling. "Not while we're still standing." He fired his air blaster, the shot hitting Ruok and causing him to stagger.

Marcus, shouted, "Keep pushing! We can beat them!"

Scarlette, her energy crackling around her, added, "For Joanna! For everyone we've lost!" She fired at another Hell Defender, her shot hitting its mark.

The battle raged on, every blast moved with precision and purpose, and every blast from his air blaster met with a calculated aim. Marcus and Scarlette fought valiantly beside him; their resolve bolstered by the sight of the citizens of London standing up against the horrors unleashed upon their city.

But then, in a horrifying moment, the tide of the battle shifted. Ruok, seeing Alex as the linchpin of the resistance, focused his malevolent power on him. With a cruel, triumphant smile, Ruok unleashed a devastating blast of dark energy.

"Alex!" Scarlette screamed, her voice echoing above the chaos.

Time seemed to slow as the blast struck Alex, lifting him off his feet and sending him crashing to the ground. The light in his eyes flickered and then went out. The air around them grew still, the noise of the battle dimming in the wake of Alex's fall.

"No!" Marcus roared, his voice filled with anguish and rage. He fired his air blaster wildly, tears streaming down his face.

Scarlette dropped to her knees beside Alex's lifeless body, her hands shaking as she reached out to him. "Alex, no..."

The citizens of London, seeing their hero fall, felt a wave of despair wash over them. The fight seemed almost futile without Alex leading them. Ruok's laugh echoed through the streets, a sound of pure, dark victory.

With a twinkle of an eye, Alex awoke, his heart pounding. He was no longer in the chaotic streets of London but in a place of ethereal beauty. He sat up, bewildered, his surroundings both familiar and strange. The palace of Esmeria stretched out before him, its golden arches and shimmering walls glowing with an otherworldly light.

"How did I get here?" Alex wondered aloud, rising to his feet.

"Welcome back, Alex," a gentle voice called out.

Alex turned to see Vesta, her eyes filled with warmth and familiarity. Beside her stood Jix, a who is a sarcastic and annoyed-easily otherworldly humanoid creature. the mischievous yet loyal companion from his past adventures, and the angelic beings Dippy and Lyra, their serene presence filling the room with light.

"Vesta... Jix... Dippy... Lyra," Alex stammered, taking in the sight of his old friends. "How am I here? I was... I was..."

Vesta stepped forward, placing a comforting hand on his shoulder. "You were in a great battle, Alex. And you fell. But do you remember the special ghost coin you obtained from the City of Illusions?"

Alex's hand instinctively went to his pocket, but it was empty. "The ghost coin... Yes, I remember."

Vesta smiled. "The coin of Resurrection. It brought you back to us. We sent it to you for this very reason."

Jix, his usual playful demeanour tempered with concern, added, "It's been a long time, Alex. It's good to see you again, even under these circumstances."

Lyra, her voice soothing and melodic, spoke softly. "You have always had a courageous heart, Alex. The coin was just a means to bring you here. Your true strength lies within you."

Dippy, his angelic wings shimmering, nodded. "Indeed, you are a true hero. The ghost coins are not the source of your power."

Alex took a deep breath, absorbing their words. "But Ruok... He's so powerful. How can I defeat him without the coin?"

Vesta's eyes sparkled with wisdom. "You have faced him before and triumphed, Alex. It was not the coin that won those battles, but your own heart and spirit. You have the power within you to defeat Ruok."

Jix grinned, his mischievous eyes twinkling. "And you won't be alone this time, mate. We're all here to help you."

Lyra placed a hand on Alex's arm, her touch comforting. "Together, we will stand against Ruok. You are not alone."

Dippy's wings unfurled slightly, his voice resolute. "We will fight by your side, Alex. Your battle is our battle."

"Thank you. All of you. I won't let you down. We will stop Ruok, together."

Vesta smiled, her eyes filled with pride. "That's the spirit, Alex. Now, let's prepare. The battle is far from over, and the people of London need their hero."

Back in London, the battle continued to rage. Marcus and Scarlette fought with a desperate fury, their grief fueling their determination. The citizens of London, seeing the bravery of their leaders, pushed back against the monsters and the IDF, their courage a beacon in the darkness.

But just as hope seemed to wane, As Alex felt the reassuring presence of his friends around him, a powerful surge of energy coursed through his veins. He looked at Vesta, whose serene eyes held a depth of wisdom. "We need to go back, Vesta," Alex said, his voice filled with determination. "London needs us."

Vesta nodded, her face reflecting the urgency of the situation. "I will transport you back, Alex. But remember, the strength you feel comes from within. Trust in it."

With a wave of her hand, a brilliant light enveloped Alex, Lyra, Dippy, and Jix. In an instant, they were transported back to the heart of the battle in London. The chaotic sounds of conflict filled their ears once more.

"Alex!" Scarlette cried out, her face lighting up with joy and relief as she saw him. "You're alive!"

Marcus, his expression a mix of shock and elation, shouted, "We thought we lost you for good!"

"I'm back. And we're going to finish this, together."

The battle resumed with renewed intensity. Alex, now imbued with the super strength he had gained from Esmeria, charged at Ruok. The two clashed in a fierce fistfight, their blows echoing like thunder through the streets of London.

Ruok's eyes glowed with malevolence as he countered Alex's attacks. "You should have stayed dead, Alex."

Alex's fists connected with Ruok's jaw, sending him staggering back. "I've come too far to let you win, Ruok. This ends now."

Meanwhile, the citizens of London, inspired by Alex's return, fought valiantly against the monsters. Marcus and Scarlette, their air blasters blazing, took down Hell Defenders with precision and fury.

"Keep pushing!" Marcus shouted, his voice a beacon of encouragement. "We're turning the tide!"

Scarlette, her face set with determination, added, "For Alex! For London!"

Lyra, her wings shimmering with ethereal light, soared above the battlefield. With a graceful motion, she unleashed beams of healing energy, mending the wounds of the brave fighters below. "Stay strong! We can do this!" she called out, her voice a soothing balm amidst the chaos.

Jix, darting through the fray with agility and speed, used his sharp claws and cunning tactics to take down several monstrous foes. "They don't stand a chance against us!" he declared, his grin mischievous yet fierce.

Dippy, his angelic presence glowing with a radiant light, channeled his celestial power to create protective barriers around the fighters, shielding them from the worst of the attacks. "We must hold the line!" he urged, his voice carrying a tone of unwavering resolve.

As the battle raged on, Mr. Ransford fought valiantly but then, in a moment of horror, Sarcum, Marcus' evil double, struck him down with a vicious blow.

"No!" Marcus screamed; his voice filled with anguish as he saw Mr. Ransford fall. The heroes stopped fighting, their faces reflecting shock and grief.

Alex, his heart aching, turned to see his fallen Teacher. "Mr. Ransford... No..."

The pause in the battle was brief, but it was enough for the reality of the situation to sink in. The loss of Mr. Ransford was a heavy blow.

The fight between Alex and Ruok intensified, their powerful blows shaking the very fabric of reality. With a sudden twist of Ruok's power, they were transported into different dimensions. Each new universe they entered was a bizarre and alien landscape, filled with dangers and challenges.

In one dimension, the sky was a swirling mass of green clouds, and the ground was a shifting sea of sand. Alex and Ruok continued their battle, their movements swift and relentless. Alex felt the strain of the endless fight, but he refused to give in. "You can't escape me, Ruok," he shouted, his voice echoing in the strange landscape.

Ruok sneered, his eyes glowing with malevolence. "Escape? This is where I thrive, Alex. You are out of your depth." With a flick of his wrist, Ruok opened another portal, and they were transported again.

This time, they found themselves in a dimension where gravity was distorted. Alex struggled to keep his footing as the ground shifted beneath him, but Ruok moved with ease, his dark energy anchoring him. "You should have stayed in your little world, Alex," Ruok taunted, his voice dripping with contempt.

As they fought on, they were pulled into yet another dimension. This one was a bleak and desolate wasteland, with a sky that burned a constant red. The air was thick with ash, and the ground was littered with the bones of long-dead creatures. Alex felt his strength waning, but he pressed on, determined not to let Ruok win.

"You are worthless, Alex," Ruok spat, his words cutting deep. "You couldn't save your mother. You can't save anyone."

Alex stumbled, the weight of Ruok's words pressing down on him. Tears filled his eyes as he remembered his mother's final moments. "No," he whispered, his voice choked with emotion. "I won't let you take everything from me."

Ruok laughed a cruel and mocking sound. "You're already defeated, Alex. Just give up."

As Alex fought to regain his strength, his eyes caught a glint of something in the distance. He saw a powerful sword embedded in the ground, its blade glowing with a fierce, fiery light. Desperation and hope surged within him. With a final burst of energy, Alex lunged for the sword.

Ruok's eyes widened as Alex grasped the hilt of the Fire Sword. "No! You can't—"

But Alex, fueled by his love for his friends and family, swung the sword with all his might. The blade cut through Ruok's defences, and Alex plunged it deep into Ruok's chest. Flames erupted from the wound, engulfing Ruok's body.

Ruok screamed, his form consumed by the fiery inferno. "This isn't over!" he roared, his voice echoing through the dimensions as he exploded into a burst of light and ash.

Back in London, the top of the Shard building began to open. A brilliant light shot up from it, piercing the dark sky. The light formed a vortex, pulling in all the monsters and evil spirits that had plagued the city. The hellish version of London began to dissolve, replaced by the familiar sights and sounds of normal life.

The citizens of London watched in awe as the light cleansed their city. "Look!" someone shouted, pointing at the sky. "The monsters are disappearing!"

As the last of the creatures were sucked into the light, the top of the Shard building closed, sealing the portal. The city was quiet once more, the horrors of the past hours fading like a bad dream.

He opened his eyes to find himself back in London, standing amidst the remnants of the battle. The city was quiet, the chaotic noise of the fight replaced by a profound silence.

For a heartbeat, Alex wondered if it was truly over. Then, a single cheer rang out, quickly followed by another and then another. The citizens of London, their faces reflecting a mix of relief, awe, and gratitude, began to cheer for Alex and his friends.

"Alex Knight! Alex Knight!" they chanted, their voices growing louder with each repetition.

Alex looked around, seeing the people who had been transformed by the mutation, now restored to their normal selves. Tears of joy and relief streamed down their faces as they embraced their loved ones. Scarlette, Marcus, Helen, Lucas Ardy, and Alex's son's friends gathered around him, their faces beaming with pride and happiness.

Scarlette stepped forward, her eyes shining. "You did it, Alex. You saved us all."

Marcus nodded, clapping Alex on the back. "You were amazing, man. We couldn't have done it without you."

Helen ran to Alex, wrapping her arms around him in a tight embrace. "I was so scared, Alex. I thought I'd lost you."

Alex hugged her back, his own eyes filled with tears. "I thought I was gone too. But we're all here. We made it."

His son rushed up to him, excitement and admiration in his eyes. "Dad, you were incredible! You are a hero!"

Alex knelt, pulling his son into a tight hug. "No, son. We all are. We fought together, and we won together."

The citizens continued to cheer, their voices a powerful testament to their collective relief and joy. Alex stood tall, feeling a profound sense of gratitude and pride. He had faced unimaginable challenges and come out victorious, but he knew it was the strength and courage of everyone around him that had made it possible.

***

Alex stood in front of his parents' grave, the weight of their loss heavy on his heart. The cool breeze rustled the leaves of the trees surrounding the cemetery, creating a peaceful, almost serene atmosphere. Helen stood beside him, her hand gently resting on his shoulder. They had brought flowers, vibrant and colourful, a stark contrast to the sombre gravestones.

He knelt, placing the flowers carefully on the grave. "Hi, Mum. Hi, Dad," he began, his voice trembling slightly. "I wish you could see us now. We've been through so much, and I miss you both every day."

Helen knelt beside him, placing her flowers next to his. "They would be so proud of you, Alex. You've done incredible things."

Alex's eyes filled with tears as he looked at the gravestone. "I just wish they were here to see it. To be part of it."

Helen wrapped her arms around him, offering comfort. "They're always with you, Alex. In your heart, in your memories. And you carry their strength with you."

Alex nodded, wiping away a tear. "I remember how Mum used to make me cheer up whenever I was feeling down. And Dad... he always had the right words to make everything seem okay."

Helen smiled, her own eyes misting with tears. "Your dad had a way with words.

They sat in silence for a moment, the memories flooding back. Alex reached into his pocket and pulled out a small photograph. It was a picture of his parents, smiling and happy. He placed it gently on the grave.

"I hope you're at peace," he whispered. "And I hope you're proud of us."

Helen squeezed his hand, her voice soft and comforting. "They are, Alex. I know they are."

A short distance away, they stood before Mr. Ransford's grave. The loss of their mentor and Teacher back in school was still fresh, and the pain of his absence was a sharp ache in their hearts. They placed flowers on his grave, their heads bowed in respect.

"You were like a father to me, Mr. Ransford," Alex said quietly. "You taught me so much. You believed in me when I didn't believe in myself."

Helen nodded, her voice filled with emotion. "You were a guiding light for all of us. We wouldn't be here without you."

Alex took a deep breath, the memories of their time together flooding his mind. "I promise to carry on your legacy. To keep fighting for what's right. To protect those who can't protect themselves."

Helen's eyes filled with tears as she looked at the grave. "Thank you, Mr. Ransford. For everything."

As they stood there, the sun began to set, casting a warm glow over the cemetery. Alex felt a sense of peace wash over him, knowing that they had honoured their loved ones' memories. He looked at Helen, his heart filled with gratitude for her unwavering support.

"We'll make them proud," he said, his voice steady and determined. "We'll keep fighting. For them. For us. For everyone."

Helen smiled, her eyes shining with love and determination. "Together, Alex. We'll do it together."

As they left the cemetery, hand in hand The transition from the chaos of London to the serene beauty of Esmeria was both abrupt and breathtaking.

Alex and his friends found themselves standing in the heart of Esmeria, surrounded by the familiar, otherworldly glow that bathed the land in perpetual twilight. The air was thick with magic, and the comforting scent of blooming flowers wafted through the air.

Vesta stood before them, her presence as commanding and graceful as ever. The citizens of Esmeria gathered around, their faces filled with admiration and gratitude.

"Welcome back, my friends," Vesta said, her voice resonating with a soothing melody. "It is always a joy to see you, though I must confess, this will be our final meeting."

Alex stepped forward, confusion and curiosity evident in his eyes. "Final meeting? What do you mean, Vesta?"

Vesta smiled gently, her eyes meeting each of theirs in turn. "You have all grown tremendously since you first set foot in Esmeria. The courage, strength, and wisdom you have gained here are now deeply rooted within you. You no longer need to return to Esmeria to find these qualities—they are a part of you, forever."

Scarlette looked around, a mix of pride and sadness in her gaze. "So, this is goodbye?"

"Not a goodbye," Vesta corrected, "but a farewell. You have completed your journey here. It is time for you to carry the light of Esmeria into your world, to continue your lives with the strength and courage you have always possessed."

As Vesta spoke, she led them through the gathered crowd to a grand plaza. There, five magnificent statues stood tall, each one a perfect likeness of Alex, Marcus, Scarlette, Alex's Stepdad Paul and Mr. Ransford.

The statues were crafted with exquisite detail, capturing not only their physical appearances but the essence of their characters.

Alex's statue stood proud and resolute, holding a sword aloft in a gesture of victory and protection. Marcus's statue exuded confidence and strength, his stance unwavering. Scarlette's statue radiated grace and power, a fierce determination in her eyes. Mr. Ransford's statue was serene and wise, a gentle smile on his lips as he watched over the others.

Alex's Stepdad, Paul, statues standing tall with a discipline smile on his face.

"These statues are evidence of your bravery and the impact you have had on Esmeria and your world," Vesta said. "They will stand here as symbols of hope and inspiration for generations to come."

Marcus's eyes shimmered with emotion as he gazed at his statue. "I never thought I'd see something like this. It's... incredible."

Scarlette nodded, tears brimming in her eyes. "We've come so far. It's amazing to see how much we've accomplished."

Vesta placed a comforting hand on Alex's shoulder. "You have all shown exceptional courage and resilience. Your legacy will live on in Esmeria, but now it is time for you to live your lives in your world."

Alex took a deep breath, a mix of pride and sadness in his heart. "Thank you, Vesta. For everything."

Vesta's eyes softened with affection. "It is we who thank you, Alex. Your courage has brought hope and light to Esmeria. You will always be remembered here."

As the citizens of Esmeria began to sing a farewell song, their voices blending in a harmonious melody, Alex and his friends stood together, holding hands. The magical light of Esmeria enveloped them, and they slowly began to fade from the realm.

The last thing Alex saw was the statues, standing tall and proud, a lasting tribute to their journey and the bonds they had forged.

***

The years had passed swiftly, and life had been kind to Alex. He sat in his spacious, comfortable office, the walls adorned with framed covers of his successful book series, "The Adventures of Alex and the Realm Defenders." and CEO of his own publishing company.

Alex leaned back in his plush leather chair, a satisfied smile playing on his lips as he glanced around the office. The space was filled with the hum of activity, the murmur of voices, and the occasional burst of laughter. It was a testament to his hard work and the unwavering support of his friends and family. His desk was cluttered with manuscripts, letters from fans, and awards, each one a reminder of the impact his stories had made.

Helen entered the office, carrying a tray with two steaming cups of coffee. She set the tray on his desk and took a seat across from him. "Busy day?" she asked, her eyes twinkling with amusement.

Alex smiled, taking a cup. "Always. But it's a good kind of busy."

Helen took a sip of her coffee, her gaze sweeping the room. "I still can't believe how far we've come. From fighting monsters to running a publishing company. It's been quite the journey."

Alex chuckled, his eyes reflecting the same disbelief and pride. "Life has a way of surprising us. But I wouldn't have it any other way."

As they talked, the door opened, and Scarlette and Marcus walked in, their faces lighting up when they saw Alex. "Hey, boss!" Marcus called out, a playful grin on his face. "Got a new manuscript for you."

Scarlette rolled her eyes, though her smile was fond. "He's been working on it non-stop. I think you're going to love it."

Alex took the manuscript, flipping through the pages. "I'm sure I will. You both have always had a knack for storytelling."

Helen had taken inspiration from the late Mr Ransford and dedicated her life to education. She became the headteacher at a local school, instilling wisdom and kindness in her students just as Mr Ransford had once done for her. Today, she stood before a group of eager young minds, discussing the importance of courage and integrity.

"Remember," she said, her voice filled with conviction, "you have the power to change the world. It all starts with believing in yourself and never giving up."

Her students nodded, their eyes wide with admiration. Helen's passion and dedication had already begun to shape the future of these young minds, much like Mr. Ransford had shaped hers.

In another part of town, Ryan and Sebastian were living their dream. They had become professional Juggle Bubble players, a sport that had gained immense popularity. Their skills and camaraderie on the field had made them stars, inspiring countless fans. On weekends, Alex and his friends would join them for friendly matches, the games filled with laughter and light-hearted competition.

"Watch this, Dad!" Ryan called out, executing a perfect bubble juggle that left everyone in awe.

Alex cheered, pride evident in his eyes. "You've got some serious skills, son. Keep it up!"

Sebastian, ever the joker, grinned. "We learned from the best!"

Ardy, now Alex's loyal pet and friend, barked excitedly from the sidelines, adding to the cheerful chaos. The bond between Alex and Ardy had only grown stronger over the years, their adventures together creating a deep sense of companionship.

Meanwhile, Marcus and Scarlette had founded an organization dedicated to using their superpowers to help those in need. Their headquarters buzzed with activity as they coordinated efforts to provide aid, protection, and hope to countless people. Lucas, having once been in a gang as a teenager, had his organization aimed at helping youth escape the cycle of violence and find better paths.

It had been a week since the launch of Alex's latest book, and life had started to settle into a new rhythm. Today was Alex's birthday, and he looked forward to a quiet evening with his family. However, when he opened the door to his house, he was greeted by a chorus of voices shouting, "Surprise!"

Alex's eyes widened in disbelief as he took in the scene before him. His friends and family filled the room, along with Lyra, Jix, Dippy, and several other magical beings from Esmeria. The house was decorated with streamers and balloons, and the air buzzed with excitement and joy.

"Happy Birthday, Alex!" Helen exclaimed, rushing forward to hug him. She had a mischievous smile on her face, clearly proud of the surprise she had orchestrated.

Alex laughed, hugging her back. "You got me this time. I had no idea!"

Ryan and Sebastian bounded over, each carrying a brightly wrapped gift. "We helped too!" Ryan said, grinning. "Wait until you see what we got you!"

Ardy, wagging his tail furiously, circled Alex's feet, clearly excited by all the commotion. "Easy, boy,"

Alex said, patting his loyal friend on the head. "There's plenty of time for fun."

Marcus, Scarlette, and Lucas approached, each holding a drink and wearing huge smiles. "Happy Birthday, old man," Marcus teased, raising his glass in a toast. "To many more adventures!"

Scarlette nodded, her eyes twinkling. "And to the best leader and friend anyone could ask for."

Lucas clinked his glass against theirs. "Here's to you, Alex.

Lyra, Jix, and Dippy floated over, their ethereal forms adding a magical touch to the celebration. Lyra smiled warmly. "It's wonderful to celebrate with you in this world, Alex. You've come so far."

Jix, always the jokester, conjured a small, glowing orb and tossed it to Alex. "Catch! It's a special birthday light from Esmeria. It'll glow brighter the happier you are."

Dippy, ever the serene presence, nodded in agreement. "You've been a beacon of hope and courage, Alex. This celebration is well-deserved."

As the party continued, Alex marvelled at the mingling of his human friends and family with the magical beings from Esmeria. There was laughter and joy, the barriers between worlds dissolving in the warmth of camaraderie. People danced to the lively music, and magical party tricks added an extra layer of enchantment to the festivities.

At one point, Ardy, excited by the array of treats, got into a bowl of fire ants meant for the Esmerians. Before anyone could stop him, he gobbled them up, his eyes wide with delight. A few moments later, his eyes widened even more, and he let out a loud, fiery fart that caused a small burst of flame to shoot out.

The room fell silent as everyone stared in shock. Ardy looked around, his tail between his legs, clearly embarrassed. Then, as if on cue, the room erupted into laughter. Alex doubled over, tears streaming down his face from laughing so hard.

"Ardy!" he managed to say between laughs. "You never fail to surprise us!"

Helen wiped away her own tears of laughter. "That's one way to light up the party!"

Ryan and Sebastian were in stitches, holding their sides. "Best. Birthday. Ever," Ryan declared, and everyone agreed.

As the evening wore on, the laughter and joy continued. Stories were shared, memories revisited, and new ones created. Alex found himself surrounded by the people he loved, each moment a reminder of how far they had come and how much they had to be grateful for.

***

London had transformed into a city where Artificial Intelligence and beings from other dimensions coexisted peacefully with humans. The skyline shimmered with futuristic buildings, and the streets buzzed with a harmonious blend of human life and advanced technology. Alex Knight's legacy paved the way for a new era of unity and collaboration.

Citizens went about their daily lives, interacting with AI companions and dimensional creatures as naturally as if they had always been part of the world. The barriers between realms had dissolved, creating a vibrant and diverse community. The city thrived, a testament to the bravery and determination of Alex and his friends.

Weeks later, a young lady sat in her cozy room, engrossed in a book about Alex Knight's adventures. The tales of heroism, courage, and unity fascinated her, filling her with a sense of wonder and curiosity. She turned the pages slowly, savoring each story, and imagining herself as part of the epic journeys.

"Can you bring up the washing?" her mother called from downstairs.

The young lady sighed, marking her place in the book and setting it aside. "Okay, Mum, I'll be right there!" she replied, reluctantly getting up. She loved losing herself in the pages of Alex Knight's adventures, but chores were a necessary part of life.

She made her way to the basement, flicking on the light as she descended the stairs. The dimly lit room was filled with the hum of the washing machine. Her mother was busy preparing to leave, her keys jangling as she gathered her things.

"I'll be out for a bit," her mother said, poking her head around the corner. "Make sure you finish the laundry and lock up. I'll be back soon."

"Got it, Mum," she replied, her voice echoing slightly in the basement. She turned her attention to the washing machine, opened the door and began to transfer the wet clothes into the laundry basket.

As she worked, her eyes were drawn to a faint glow emanating from a dark corner of the basement. Curious, she set down the laundry basket and walked over to investigate. There, partially hidden beneath a layer of dust, was a book. It looked old and slightly burnt, its edges sang as if it had survived a fire.

She reached out and picked it up, blowing away the dust to reveal the title: "Guide to Worlds." Her heart skipped a beat. She had heard of this book from the stories of Alex Knight, but she had never imagined she would find it in her basement.

She carefully opened the book, the pages crackling slightly with age. As she read the magical words inscribed within, the glow intensified. Suddenly, a portal began to form, swirling with vibrant colours and pulsing with energy.

The young lady's eyes widened in amazement as the portal grew larger, filling the basement with a mesmerizing light. She stepped back, feeling a mixture of fear and excitement. The portal beckoned to her, promising adventures beyond her wildest dreams.

"What is this?" she whispered to herself, her heart pounding in her chest. She glanced back at the stairs, half expecting her mother to reappear and call her back to reality. But the basement remained quiet, the only sound the soft hum of the portal.

THE END